"Full of heart and a strong sense of sisterhood, *In the Heart of Paradise* is **guaranteed to please readers who love women-centric stories featuring strong and independent women.** McGillen touches upon mental health issues such as anxiety and depression and gives an accurate portrayal of how those issues were handled in the 19th century."
—Pikasho Deka, *Readers' Favorite*

# IN THE HEART OF PARADISE

*The Rainier Series, Book 3*

## JAMIE MCGILLEN

The
Evergreen
Bookshelf

THE RAINIER SERIES, BOOK 3

# IN THE HEART OF PARADISE

## JAMIE MCGILLEN

*"You gain strength, courage, and confidence by every experience in which you really stop to look fear in the face. You are able to say to yourself, 'If I have lived through this horror, I can take the next thing that comes along.' You must do the thing you think you cannot do."*

—Eleanor Roosevelt

*"Nothing thicker than a knife's blade separates happiness from melancholy."*

—Virginia Woolf

# CONTENTS

# FOREWORD
## BY RICHELLE MARRACINO, MD

Life is full of challenges, particularly for women. We struggle to overcome the circumstances of our lives, to achieve something better for ourselves and those we love.

I know, because I've been there personally. And in my twenty-something years as a physician and life coach, I've had the breathtaking privilege of being there for other women as they reach their goals. We're all recovering from something. Be it a physical ailment, mental health issue, learning disability, or social stigma, we've all been sidelined by life in some way. When the sleepless nights are too many and the ache is unbearable, a little encouragement can go a long way. We all need to know we're not alone and we're going to make it.

This long upward battle is not unlike climbing a mountain. The same way we prepare our gear for a physical climb, before embarking on our inner journey, we must shake loose the inherent fear or shame accompanying the challenge. We have to reject society's expectations—the messages locking us into quiet predictability—and hold true to our belief in ourselves.

Throughout the climb, we must gather the resolve to tackle the insurmountable, the courage and tenacity to press on despite the perils, setbacks, and discouragement. We often chart our course with nothing resembling a map. All we have is our internal compass, determination to summit, and the audacity to dream that it's possible. That's the stuff we're made of as women.

To this day, women remain underrepresented among mountaineers. But when it comes to overcoming challenges, we are all out there braving the elements. We're all scattered across the face of the mountain, inching our way toward the summit. My hope is that we stay connected and roped to each other, because none of us can get there alone.

This message comes through with boldness and clarity in Jamie McGillen's much-anticipated third novel of her ongoing Rainier series. Strength for the journey is woven into every page. In her first book, *In Sight of the Mountain*, we're introduced to Anna Gallagher, a nineteen-year-old who pursues her dream of climbing the icy peak of Mount Rainier. She risks it all, including her family, society's approval, and the esteem of the man she loves. Anna's story continues in the second book, *In Light of the Summit*, as she reaps the consequences of being a female trailblazer in the late 19th century. She faces shame, ridicule, and threats as she fearlessly broadens the horizon for women climbers.

In this third book of the series, the author draws us deeper into Anna's world and that of her friends, bringing us right into their parlors, kitchens, and bedrooms. Their fears, secrets, longings, and dreams are utterly relatable, despite being set over a hundred years ago. The characters live, laugh, and breathe off the page. We take a front seat to their struggles, witnessing their heartbreak and their triumphs.

Although fictional, McGillen's characters are worthy emblems of the real women who paved the way before us. They faced the grit of daily life, undeterred. They balked against societal restrictions and lived to tell. They empower and inspire us to challenge our limiting beliefs and never give up. Most of all, they remind us to pay it forward for generations of women to come.

American popular science and humor writer, Mary Roach, wrote, "Heroism doesn't always happen in a burst of glory. Sometimes small triumphs and large hearts change the course of history."

The women in McGillen's book are like you and me. They love and hurt deeply. They dare greatly. They refuse to let society's expectations define them. They push themselves out of their comfort zone and accomplish more than they thought possible. They plant their flag at their peak and call us to do the same. They harken the voice of a female author of that age, Helen Keller, who reminds us, "Life is either a daring adventure or nothing. To keep our faces toward change and behave like free spirits in the presence of fate is strength undefeatable."

The women in this book whisper to us: May you find your daring adventure and live it fully to the end. Get your crampons, rope in, and climb on! You're in for an empowering ride.

—Richelle Marracino, MD
richellemarracino.com

# PROLOGUE
## THE PAST

*Elizabeth | September 1885*

lizabeth Grayson paused as the music of her violin vibrated beyond the last note. With her eyes closed, she let the reverberations wash away her uneasiness.

She drew the red velvet curtains slightly to peer out the window into the rainy street. In the silence, only the soft rain made its presence known against the pane.

The shouting from next door had finally ceased, but she couldn't get the terror out of her chest or the metallic taste out of her mouth.

Mrs. Hampton, the eccentric woman who had lived on their road for Elizabeth's entire life, had made all kinds of ruckus while two men dragged her away. The woman had always been odd, but Elizabeth would have never imagined that she was prone to hysterics, as her husband claimed.

He had been shouting over her cries for help. *"Being in an institution will calm your nerves, dear. Maybe even silence the voices you hear."*

Elizabeth shuddered at the idea of hearing voices. Ever since she'd learned that this condition existed, she feared that she might hear them one day too.

Without looking down, she could feel her corset, and she despised its stiffness. The rough fabric against her skin, pressing against her breasts that wouldn't stop growing. And now that she was nearly thirteen, she couldn't get away with childish pinafores.

Her starched petticoats made her legs itch, or rather gave the sensation of an itch, but it was under her skin, something that crawled underneath.

As she returned her violin to its case, she wondered if anyone had ever watched her leave the house. Often, she returned to her front door after leaving to make sure she had locked it. Going back, again and again to stare at it, then touch it one last time, and then another. It was certainly an odd thing to do, but the alternative—fearing all day that she'd left it unlocked, or even left the door wide open—would make it impossible to focus on her studies.

Just imagining someone witnessing this ridiculous scene gave her a flash of panic. Every muscle in her body froze until they ached. She lowered herself into a chair, trying to catch her breath.

Surely it was normal for people to check their locks. But if anyone realized it was a daily obsession for her—something that could consume her mind if she let it—that would raise suspicions.

Her nerves were like frayed tendons poking out from a

wound. She feared the day that she wouldn't be able to hide it any longer.

She had heard of women who became progressively madder as they got older, some starting as young as she was. First, the doctors would come and try to help. Next, they would send them to a sanctuary of some sort that sought to bring their health back. But eventually, if they didn't improve, the man to whom they belonged—husband or father—would admit them to a hospital for the insane.

But Elizabeth was too smart to end up like that. Even if she deserved to be there because of her weak constitution. There was a fine line between a fainting lady and a crazy woman. And it was typically the men, along with handpicked doctors, who would decide on which side of the line any woman might fall.

She would need to be careful.

If she was lucky enough to make it to adulthood without going mad or becoming institutionalized, she hoped to become a nurse like Florence Nightingale. The orderliness and cleanliness of hospitals calmed her. Everything had a place, and everyone had a job to do—and it was important. Double-checking things would be a virtue.

Someone knocked on the door, and Elizabeth glanced nervously toward the front entrance. It was a deep oak piece that she'd always admired, but she rarely enjoyed crossing its threshold. With a lump of nervousness in her throat, she feared it was the police or a doctor coming for her next. But she forced herself to leave the comfort of the sitting room and open that heavy door to the outside world.

The wind brought in the scent of damp earth.

"Did you see that?" the brown-haired girl asked, sweeping a wet strand of hair to the side of her face.

Everyone who lived on their street had heard the commotion.

"Yes, it's awful." Elizabeth folded her arms over her chest.

"I've always thought Mrs. Hampton peculiar, but I didn't know she was suffering so much. Hopefully, they can cure her. Do you suppose?"

"Perhaps they should have just let her be," Elizabeth responded after a long pause.

The girl shrugged. "Seems like she kept getting more dangerous—I've heard there's a point of madness you can't return from."

Elizabeth swallowed uncomfortably, wondering if the girl could sense the fear in her eyes. "Anyway, I need to finish my chores."

The girl gave her a peculiar look and then waved silently as she turned to walk away.

Once Elizabeth was back in the sitting room, she sank into an overstuffed chair, bringing her knees to her chest and hugging them.

The entire world was unsafe, and there was a part of herself that needed to remain hidden. A fragile, precious side of herself that she must never share, not even with a friend. It would be far too dangerous.

# CHAPTER ONE
## THE TELEGRAM

*Elizabeth | June 1891*

As she read Levi's message, Elizabeth froze. An unexpected sting of pain coiled in her belly, squeezing her insides.

The telegram slipped from her stiff hands and floated to the wood floor below.

The weakness in her legs surprised her, so she lowered herself onto a wooden trunk. Her tongue felt like rough wool against the roof of her mouth. She knew this feeling and hoped it wouldn't turn into a full-blown episode of panic.

The words jumped from the slip of paper to play a loop in her mind.

*- I AM IN LOVE WITH ANOTHER WOMAN.*
*I AM SO SORRY. LETTER TO FOLLOW. -*

Perhaps she should have seen this coming. Their courtship may not have lasted much longer anyway, but she had grown accustomed to the way things had been: having someone to write to, a man to think about.

But it would have only been a matter of time until Levi realized how odd she truly was.

Elizabeth pressed her damp palms onto her cool cotton skirts. She wiggled her toes to make sure she could trust her legs to carry her.

Not yet.

Perhaps Levi had sensed something was off with her. She certainly hadn't been a polite guest when she'd visited the Gallaghers. Always stumbling over her words and slinking away from eye contact, keeping her secrets hidden. His family was so . . . . joyful and free. She would have never fit in with them anyway.

The shouts of the children playing around her brought her back to the present with a jolt. She'd been staying at her aunt's house going on two months, and they were quite used to her.

"What's it say?" asked her yellow-haired cousin with round eyes.

"We must talk in proper sentences during the school day, mustn't we?" Elizabeth scolded without looking up.

The little girl cleared her throat. "What does the note say, Miss Elizabeth?"

Pulling herself together, she stood from the trunk of toys, smoothing her white cotton shirt, and lifted her chin. The message proved that Levi preferred a sane woman, someone better socially equipped than she, but she only said, "Never mind, dear. It's private."

With a spin of her heel, she plucked the telegram from the

ground and tucked it into a pocket in her skirt. As she left the room, tears stung her eyes.

Levi had been good to her for the few months they'd been courting. But he must not have liked her reticence and the way she refused to open up as a normal lady would. She probably seemed aloof to him. That was likely the gist of the forthcoming letter, and she couldn't bear to read it.

What had she been thinking, letting someone get close to her? It was her own fault for accepting the offer of courtship, and yet what a joy it had been to be wanted.

But perhaps with marriage out of the realm of possibilities, she could focus on becoming a nurse like she'd wanted to do since she was a girl of twelve.

She had so enjoyed taking care of her aunt during the births of her other two children, and during her lying-in times after. Every time she'd assisted her aunt, she'd learned something new.

Having a task to do calmed her nerves, giving her a purpose to immerse herself in. And if she was lucky, becoming a nurse in a hospital would calm her mind in the same way that music did.

But at the moment, there were children to tend to and her pregnant aunt to help as she endured the final weeks before her babies were due—twins. The doctor believed it to be so based on the size of her stomach and the sound of two heartbeats. They had just discovered this last week, and the house was abuzz with excitement at the turn of events. And her aunt was nervous about the delivery.

Keenly aware of the slip of paper in her pocket, shame from the rejection burned Elizabeth's cheeks. Absentmindedly, she followed the scent of baked bread into the kitchen where Aunt Rose Marie stood at the cookstove. The news from this telegram was hers alone for the time being, so she did her best to make her face cheery.

"Let me do that," she said, scooting her aunt toward the kitchen table with gentle pressure. "Rest a moment."

"You're too good to me, darling." Aunt Rose Marie lowered herself onto a chair and reached for a piece of warm bread. "Have you been able to find anything in those books about delivering two babies at once?"

Elizabeth washed her hands in the basin of water in the kitchen and then dried them on a stiff towel hanging next to the cookstove. But when she wiped the last of the droplets away, her instincts told her that her hands weren't clean at all. Lost in thought as she'd been while washing, she had probably done a poor job. Without looking up, she began scrubbing again. "Yes, I did read about it, and you'll be perfectly safe. Try not to worry."

Each finger needed a thorough cleansing. And if the top layer of skin was purged in the process, that was a sacrifice she was willing to make. The alternative would be unbearable.

Her aunt tilted her head, watching her, and let out a frazzled breath before finally saying, "You'll make a fine nurse, my dear."

The warmth of the stove and her aunt's kindness washed away what she already knew was illogical panic about dirty hands. The numbness in her arms receded, and then the sensation of pins and needles covered her hands as she dried them once more.

She offered a small smile. "I hope to become one someday."

It would give her a purpose for her life, especially now that Levi had released her from a courtship that should never have been.

"Was the telegram from your mother? I expect she's well."

Elizabeth nodded but steeled her face as she reached for her own piece of bread. Levi might as well have etched his words in a gold bar for how heavy the letter felt in her skirts. "Mother is fine. She sends her love. My brother will come to accompany me home a few weeks after the babies are born."

"I'm so happy for you to return to Seattle and back to your own life. But, truly, what am I going to do without you?"

"You'll be just fine. I'm sure of it." Elizabeth took a bite of bread and savored the toasty goodness.

"It's a relief that you'll be here for the birthing. Truth be told, I'm anxious as an unmilked cow. And my lying-in will be the hardest I've had yet, what with two babies. I'm getting too old for childbearing."

Elizabeth smiled, grateful to be appreciated and glad to be of service.

But then her thoughts turned back to Levi, and her stomach soured. It would have been far more difficult to get this news while looking into his gentle eyes as his rough hand rested softly on hers.

*Yes. It's all for the best.*

"Alright, that's enough of a rest for me. Would you mind playing a song on your violin while I finish up?"

Elizabeth wiped her hands on a rag again to make sure all the moisture was gone and then turned toward her violin case in the corner. With a graceful motion, she reached inside the velvet and pulled out her beloved instrument that always made everything better. Not the wood itself, but the beautiful music that sprang forth.

She put the polished chestnut instrument to her chin, letting the cool of the wood settle into her bones. Lifting the bow into place, she closed her eyes.

In an instant, she was at peace. The resonant minor key and the vibrations in the air seemed to still every cell in her body. The structure of the notes and rests put her at ease. Music required precise actions. Her mind, that usually worked faster than a steam engine, became tranquil and light— nothing else mattered.

The last note vibrated the air until silence surrounded her. It was but a temporary reprieve from her burdens, but she was grateful for the moment.

Later that evening, in solitude, she plunged her hands into the washbasin and scrubbed with rose-scented soap until her skin stung.

It felt good—the washing. During the act, there was hope that she might actually feel clean when she finished. But inevitably there would be a sense of dread—of "not quite" clean, the reason being just beyond her comprehension.

If only she could keep the ailments of her mind a secret, she might become a proper nurse. But if she wasn't careful, someone could institutionalize her even sooner than she'd ever feared.

# CHAPTER TWO
## MORE REAL THAN MEMORY

*Anna | September 1891*

Anna's fingers were as cold as the glaciers beneath her. They tingled as she hiked upward. Night was falling, but she pressed on, hoping to make it to the summit before the snow started. The stars shone where the clouds parted, but the darkness drew lower by the minute. Her breath was a puff of whiteness in the indigo world around her, and even the ice below was turning a purplish hue.*

*It would be a magical sight if not for the fact that Peter was watching her from far above. The weight of his gaze made her feet heavy, the crampons sticking in the ice, refusing to come out without a fight. The slower she moved, the more menacing his eyes became.*

As the darkness above faded into something lighter, the edges crumbled ominously until, finally, she woke up, covered in sweat and out of breath.

It took a moment for her to realize it had been a dream,

and even when she was sure of the reality of her surroundings in her bedroom, the nightmare still felt more real than any memory.

Ben breathed softly beside her, and the full moon shone in the clear sky outside the window. Judging by the color of the horizon, it would be morning soon. There was no chance of getting back to sleep now, so she rose.

Her stomach had been unsettled for days, and these recurring nightmares just made her feel even more out of sorts. She tied her robe, welcoming the comfort of the soft weight on her shoulders. The cold hardwood under her feet both grounded her and put a chill inside her. She found her slippers, grateful for the extra layer between her and the unforgiving floor.

It was Peter who had cut her safety rope and shoved her down the mountain. It was he who had also put Ben's life in peril as they both tumbled down the rocky mountain toward the deep crevasse below. And yet he had escaped without punishment, and he was out there somewhere near.

Any day, he might show up as he had the very first night she'd been at base camp, all alone in her tent. His shadow looming while he fumbled with her tent strings, while she clutched the whale-bone knife Ben had given her.

In the living room, the fluffy puppy lifted his little head to watch her moving toward the hearth. The dim light of the predawn morning cast an eerie glow on the brick fireplace and the shelves of books that surrounded it.

"Good morning, Comma," she said as she lit the candles on the mantel and then stoked the fire.

She scooped him up into her arms, knowing there would only be a few weeks left of him being small enough. His soft head nestled into her neck, and she breathed in his fresh puppy breath.

Anna walked out into the cool morning and set him down to explore. A peculiar ambiance colored the day—her mood, normally steady, seemed off-kilter. And it wasn't simply because of her nightmares.

Perhaps it was the full moon?

Or maybe her courses were due soon?

Yes, that was it. Any day now, she would have to endure the week of the month that made it difficult to be a woman. Which would be just fine, because in two weeks, she was due to meet Fay Fuller at base camp to discuss the women's mountaineering team. The timing would be excellent.

Back inside, she pulled out her leather journal and looked to previous pages to decipher exactly how soon she should expect the blessed event.

Anna stopped short when she saw that the last time had been just before their trip to Mount Rainier. The fortunate timing had been a relief, as she'd been unencumbered for the entirety of the journey.

But that was nearly six weeks ago. Her heart sank into her stomach as a small laugh escaped from her lips.

Could it be true?

Could she be with child?

She'd always imagined she would know at once. How could one not notice that a soul had come to join one's own? With a hand to her stomach, she smiled.

It had always been her plan to become a mother, but now did not feel like the ideal time. It had only been a year since their union, and they hadn't yet taken all the adventures they planned to.

Perhaps her cycle was just off because of the great effort of climbing the mountain. She didn't want to make assumptions and definitely didn't want to tell Ben before she knew for certain.

Plus, she'd need to plan something special. That's what he would do, and he always made things more fun. She decided to visit Heather that morning, since Ben had the day off from the mill and would likely sleep in as long as he could.

Heather could tell her how to know for sure, so she wouldn't get Ben excited over nothing. Perhaps she needed to see a doctor first before having certainty. She'd never been in a household with a pregnant woman. The only experience that came close had been with June, but she'd missed the whole first part of the time June had been expecting. She smiled, thinking of how well her dear friend was doing down in California with such an odd choice for a husband as Dr. Connor Evans.

She closed her journal and returned to the bedroom to dress without waking Ben. It was a shame she couldn't wear pants in everyday life, but the weight of skirts was something she knew all too well.

After taking off her cream-colored nightdress, she put on a simple calico and braided her long, dark hair in a loose French braid.

It would probably be best to bring Comma so that he wouldn't make a racket and wake Ben, plus Pisha loved to play with him. The two of them had enough energy for an entire pack of mules.

After leaving Ben a note, she gathered her things and the puppy and set off toward the house Heather shared with her husband in town. The early morning air was crisp. Shiny beads of water clung to blades of grass and morning glories that vined over stone walls.

The city trees that lined the street were bright with life and green foliage. Soon, September would slip into true autumn, and the street would boast a colorful display which would add a delicious crunch to every step as the trees shed their leaves.

She tapped softly on Heather's front door so as not to wake anyone if they were still sleeping. Comma whined, knowing exactly where they were. His whole body wagged along with his tail for the little girl who gave him her full attention.

Soon, Heather came to the small window beside the door, peeking through the lace eyelet curtain to see who had come to visit. She smiled when she saw Anna and whisked her inside at once.

"Well, good morning," Heather said in a hushed voice.

"Is everyone else still sleeping? Perhaps another time—"

"It's fine. Pisha will be up any minute, and I see you've brought her friend."

Anna laughed as Heather bent down to ruffle Comma's head.

"Can I get you some coffee?" Heather asked.

"Please. That would be wonderful."

"Make yourself at home. I was just getting some bread started." Heather wiped her hands with a rough-looking towel looped around her belt.

As the water boiled for coffee, Anna decided she couldn't wait another moment before sharing her delightful secret.

"I think I might be with child."

Heather spun around with a grin. "That's wonderful!"

"Well, I *think* I might be. I thought you could tell me how I'm to know for certain."

"Honestly, I'm a little disappointed I didn't notice already," Heather said with a frown. "But no matter. How late are you?"

"Two weeks."

Heather grinned. "Yes, I'd say you're likely with child—in the second month. How have you been feeling?"

"Mostly fine, I believe. I've had some nightmares the last few nights."

Heather added ground roasted coffee beans to a kettle of water. As it began to boil, the rich scent filled the room. Anna had been looking forward to the hot cup since she'd woken up, but now the smell made her stomach turn.

"I'm sorry about the bad dreams. Do you want to talk about them?"

"No. Thank you, though."

She thought of Peter and wondered what had become of him. Ben had spoken with the police as soon as they'd returned from their trip. The police chief, Emily's father, had assured him they would do everything they could to find him.

But that had been weeks ago, and there had been no trace of him anywhere in Seattle.

There had been evidence of arson in the ashes of the Gallagher bookstore. But, if he had already fled the area, Anna knew he'd probably never have to answer for his actions.

"I guess I have a little nausea too," she said as Heather set a cup of coffee in front of her. "Actually, I'm not even sure if I'll be well enough to go to the library association meeting this afternoon."

"And have you ever been this late before?"

"No. Not like this. I lost track of the weeks after getting back from the mountain, and then there was the visit to California."

"It makes me glad that you could see June. I'm delighted that she has a home and family now." Heather smiled and put her hands on her hips. "Well, congratulations."

Anna expected genuine joy to settle in her chest, like the

sun resting on sparkling snow. But she wasn't sure how she felt about being with child.

"It's not great timing, really." She paused. "We have a planned trip back up to base camp to meet with Fay in a couple of weeks. Do you suppose that would be alright, considering this turn of events?"

She couldn't bring herself to be more descriptive about her condition. Not just yet.

"I suppose that's up to you and Ben."

Anna nodded. "Of course."

She hesitated again, opening her mouth and then letting it fall closed.

"Is everything all right?" Heather asked, putting a hand on Anna's arm.

"I feel I can tell you this, but I'm afraid it might betray something unseemly in my nature. I only tell you because you're such a good friend, and I hope you won't think less of me."

"Of course, you can say anything."

Anna took a deep breath. "It seems too soon to have a child. Ben and I are so happy with our lives exactly as they are. And I'm afraid that starting a family will change so much. Will I still be able to pursue climbing or travel outside the city?"

Heather nodded slowly with understanding. "It's normal to be worried about these things. You will figure it all out in time. And Ben is a good man. He'll help you through."

Anna looked down at her hands. They were strong, and she was tough. It would take more than a pregnancy and becoming a mother to stop her.

Wouldn't it?

"If my grandmother were still with us, she'd be delighted for you." Heather glanced out the window with a look of longing, as if her grandmother was somewhere along the horizon, across the bay with her tribe. "And she would have been a fine midwife for you. I'll do the best I can, though, and perhaps a doctor or midwife can come as well."

"You'll do fine." Anna put her hand on her friend's arm and squeezed gently. "You learned so much from Kiyotsa. She'd be so proud of you."

Heather wiped a tear from the corner of her eye before it fell. "I'm not sure how she'd feel about us living here in town. I'm not even sure how I feel about it."

"How has everything been going?"

"I don't belong, but that's exactly what I expected. Pisha has made some friends, but some mothers don't let their children play with her. It's like a strike across my face."

"I'm sorry." Anna had been trying to help her friend get comfortable in the city, but she still didn't know how best to do so.

"I'm afraid to be in town after dark, even when Michael is with me. He has assured me that the police heavily discourage the old unspoken laws. But there are still those who would delight in bringing harm to the Duwamish."

Anna nodded, holding the warm mug in her hands. "Will you send Pisha to school when the time comes?"

With a deep sigh, Heather settled back into her seat. "Michael believes she should go. But I'm not so sure. What do you think?"

Anna thought back to her first year in grade school. It was when she had met Emily and June, a time of magic and learning to read and feeling like part of the town she had just moved to. Her Irish accent had faded when her classmates had difficulties understanding her. She'd figured out quickly how to fit in with the other little girls in the class.

Had that been a good thing?

It had led to good things—she knew that for certain. It was a bittersweet memory, which had brought her down a path to a life she now loved.

"Maybe Pisha should decide."

Heather nodded.

Later, as Anna walked home, she reflected on her situation. Just because she was with child, that didn't mean she couldn't stay active and enjoy the outdoors as much as ever. She'd heard that fresh air was great for a growing babe and the mother.

But how would becoming a mother change her?

Would she be able to accomplish all the things she still had in her heart, or would her condition restrict her to being stuck at home after everything she'd accomplished?

# CHAPTER THREE
## THE TRAIN TO SEATTLE

*Elizabeth*

After changing into an appropriate dress for travel, Elizabeth gathered her toilette. She placed her straw hat decorated with lilacs over her hair, then checked her reflection in the mirror that hung over the padded leather bench in the foyer. The purple scarf of striped silk on her neck looked fashionable with the hat.

An oversized gray and white vase held an assortment of roses and peonies, so she plucked the freshest rose and pinned it to her bosom. The fresh scent gave her vitality.

The entire family had gathered to say farewell. She kissed Aunt Rose Marie on the cheek and hugged her cousins goodbye. Then she caressed the soft faces of the newborns.

Her niece and nephew had tears in their eyes. They were desperate to keep their cousin with them somehow—knowing just how consumed their mother would be with those babies while their father left the house for work every day.

"You children must obey your mother," she commanded, but her face was soft. Tearing herself from all the little ones felt unnatural. "I should take my leave. My brother ought to have my things loaded by now."

She shut the door solidly, then turned back around to double-check its integrity. She stared at it for a moment, the nerves of the departure making her actions that much more insufferable. One last time, she reached for the handle, for the reassuring touch that proved it was properly closed, and then she made herself turn on her heel to hurry down the steps.

When she came to the carriage, her brother, James, gave her a sympathetic expression. It made her cheeks warm.

Had he seen her check the door?

Twice?

She imagined he was thinking her behavior odd, but perhaps he only thought of how sad she must be to leave their relatives behind again.

He offered his arm without a word and helped her into the carriage that would take them and her trunk to the train station.

As she looked out the window at the bustling city, she glanced again at her brother. He knew about her odd behaviors, but he also knew to keep them secret. All the same, whenever someone caught her doing something strange, it seemed as if she stood on the stage of a play naked, and everyone was gawking at her freckled skin. As if she needed one more pitying look to crush her fragile self-worth into the finest of powders.

Luckily, no one knew how bad things got for her in private, not even her brother. She tried her very best to act properly and unconcerned about her obsessions when she was out and about.

When they arrived at the train depot, a cacophony of sounds greeted her ears. A train whistled as it pushed away from the platform, and black smoke poured around it. A conductor shouted something before hopping into an open door of a train car. The clanging of metal against metal made her teeth hurt, and she longed to cover her ears like a child might. Even the low mumble of conversation and strangers' voices surrounding them on the platform overwhelmed her senses.

When their train arrived, James held his hand to aid her up the questionable steps and then turned back to help load the trunk.

Later, when they found seats inside, she sighed in relief, letting her muscles relax. Then she pulled out the apple she had slipped into her bag.

The sweet crispness of the fruit was a relief from the smoky atmosphere of the train car. After she had enjoyed every bite, she wrapped the apple core in her handkerchief and pulled out her book.

"What are you reading, sister?" James asked, leaning back in his seat and resting one foot on his other knee.

"It's called *Introductory Notes on Lying-in Institutions* by Florence Nightingale."

"Ahh, I see. Didn't get enough experience with the birth of twins and your aunt's lying-in period? Or the many other births you've attended?"

Elizabeth laughed. Her brother always put her at ease, even when he was teasing her. He knew what to ignore and what things to tease about, which made all the difference.

"I have so much more to learn. This has been published

for nearly twenty years, and we still don't have an institution in the west for training midwifes and midwifery nurses."

"And you shall remedy that, I hope," he said with a grin.

"I think it would be marvelous to be a nurse like her. When we arrive home, I plan to ask Dr. Glazier if I might join him the next time he attends a birth. Or some other home visit where a nurse would be of service."

"You could ask Mother if any of her friends will give birth soon. Or have ailing parents that need attending to," he said. "Or volunteer at one of the new hospitals."

"Those are excellent ideas." She smiled gratefully at him.

He nodded once, with a gracious flourish of his hand, as if to agree with her.

The train rumbled on until they were nearly at the Tacoma station. The piercing whistle sounded as they pulled up to the wooden platform.

After a quick stop, the train lurched on, and two men around Levi's age hurried past them down the aisle.

She had done her best not to think of him anymore. He'd been the first man to fancy her. Most of the boys she'd gone to school with thought her odd. When Levi had asked to court her, she'd been over the moon and had let her guard down.

She had received his letter a few weeks after the telegram had arrived. He had been in love with this other woman since they were children—it hadn't even been about her after all. He'd mentioned her name—Emily—and she'd immediately known it was Anna's friend who she'd met previously and then seen again at Anna's wedding.

Imagining Levi and Emily together made her stomach sink, although she knew it shouldn't. Her mind was on a loop, like waves beating against her that she couldn't stop. As she leaned her forehead on the glass pane of the window, a man in a brown suit slipped into the seat across from her brother, nodding politely at both of them.

"Sir and miss, I do hope you aren't holding this seat for someone even later than I."

James shook his head and smiled. "Of course not. You're more than welcome. I'm James Grayson, and this is my sister, Miss Elizabeth Grayson."

Elizabeth's muddled mind released her at once. The man's dark brown hair was combed neatly, as was fashionable, and his suit was tailored nicely.

She mustered a smile and put her gloved hand out to him, which he quickly took with a small bow of his head and chest. As he let go of her hand to shake her brother's, a tingle of relief flowed through her.

"Pleased to meet you both. I'm North Bailey," he said in a friendly manner. "I'm not always late for my engagements, I assure you."

"And which stop shall be yours?" James asked, settling back into his seat.

"Back to Seattle for me. I'm actually driving the next train south. Must have misread the schedules."

Elizabeth furrowed her brow. "Do you mean you're a train conductor? And your given name is North?"

"That's right, miss. On both accounts." He pulled a newspaper out of his small brown satchel and set it on his lap.

"How delightful," she replied, glancing at her brother, who seemed intrigued with the man sitting across from them.

"Yes, I agree. What luck to be seated next to a man who knows how to run these magnificent trains. I'm quite sure I have plenty to ask you," James said.

Elizabeth looked out the window again as the men discussed the inner workings of the engines. The scenery was beautiful, as always, but she kept stealing glances at the dark-haired man with the newspaper on his lap.

After a while, silence settled over them, and Mr. Bailey looked down at his paper while her brother busied himself with writing notes in his notebook, presumably about how train engines worked.

By the time they reached the Seattle station, she'd stolen far too many glances at the man and felt a blush come over her face when he caught her.

"Mr. Bailey, I don't believe you've flipped a single page of that paper."

The man's face tightened, and he fumbled as he closed the newspaper, then put it under his arm.

A lightning surge of panic jolted through her. It had been a foolish thing to say. It would have been better if she'd said nothing.

"Good to meet you both," he said with a nod, then stood and turned away from her before the train came to a complete stop.

She felt ill for making such a senseless comment, which had clearly been inappropriate. It had flustered the poor man. Perhaps he appreciated the article he had read and wanted to read it twice. Or maybe he had been intent on solving a difficult crossword puzzle. Either way, it was surely none of her business.

And that was one of the many reasons she kept her mouth shut around strangers. Who knew what silly thing she would say to embarrass herself or others? She would have liked to sink into the depths of the earth.

Angrily, she sighed, then glanced over at her brother.

He stood and tapped Mr. Bailey on the shoulder. "What a pleasure meeting you, sir. If you ever want to come by our house for dinner sometime, I'd love to continue the conversation. Here's our address right here."

He slipped a note to Mr. Bailey with a grin.

With a final nod, the handsome man left as quickly as he'd come, and Elizabeth was quite sure he wasn't ever planning to call on them.

❦

WHEN ELIZABETH WAS FINALLY in her own bedroom at her father's house, she relaxed. She'd been gone for quite some time, and although she'd had a wonderful visit with her aunt and cousins, there was nothing like home.

She had changed little about her room decorations since she was a young girl.

Drapery adorned the bedstead, giving the room a soft ambiance. On the ceiling, a small white hoop fastened with a brass chain held the pretty pink material—light and airy. The fabric draped over both sides of her bed, hanging in two waterfalls of cloth.

From the same soft pink material, her mother had sewn ruffles on the hems of the canopy, with a white satin ribbon tying each side back against the bedstead.

She walked over to her dressing table, which sat next to her bed with a mirror suspended above it. Bracket candlesticks made of brass hung on either side, giving her reflection a soft glow. Elizabeth took down her blond hair and brushed it until it glistened in the candlelight. Each hair pin had its own place in the ivory bowl on the dressing table.

Her mother had filled the pitcher in her washstand, and so she poured it into the bowl and washed the grime of travel off her face and neck. A clean cotton cloth hung from the side of the stand, which she used to dry herself.

The coolness of the water had awakened her, but her legs were weak beneath her from the long day of travel.

As she slipped into her nightdress and blew out the candles in her room, the full weight of everything that was happening in her life settled upon her.

It was better to think of it this way: she was no longer encumbered with a suitor. She ought not get too close to anyone anyhow and expose how frayed her nerves could become. It was better to keep to herself and pursue her childhood desires of following in the footsteps of Florence Nightingale.

It would be vital for people to see her as a sensible lady, ready and able to care for the ailing or those bearing children.

This was how she could remain safe—being a helpful and intelligent lady—a nurse who blended into the background of more important matters. Keeping to herself and having a little mystery probably wouldn't raise any concern, and it would allow her to stay safely out of reach of anyone who tried to get too close.

# CHAPTER FOUR
## SWEDISH PANCAKES AND GOOD NEWS

*Anna | September 1891 | The Second Month*

Ben rested his hand on Anna's belly as sunshine poured into their bedroom.

"Do you hope for a boy or a girl?" he asked.

She smiled. "I'll never tell. Either would be wonderful."

With a laugh, he rolled out of bed. "Let me get some breakfast started. You wait right there, Mrs. Chambers."

She sat up and rested her back against the oak headboard with a smile. As if her husband could get any more endearing. When she'd told him the news, he had shouted with joy. His enthusiasm had helped her inch toward excitement herself, but she still wasn't as over the moon as she thought she'd be when with child.

She recalled the words of Ben's mother that fateful day

when they'd first met and had been discussing climbing the mountain.

*"Won't you be with child by summer?"*

She had asked because the condition would prove self-limiting. It would have made hiking higher than base camp impossible.

And how else would being with child limit her?

The sound of pots clanging in the kitchen made her think of Greta and her grandfather, and she smiled as she imagined telling her family about the baby at Sunday brunch later. Her brother and his wife, Emily, would be there as well, which would make it even more delightful. She must keep her spirits up. A baby was always a good thing—that's what Greta said.

A few minutes later, Ben returned with peppermint tea and toast—the only things that didn't sour her stomach lately.

"You spoil me."

He kissed her cheek and then strolled toward the door again.

"Wait, can we talk about the trip to meet with Fay?"

"Sure. What are you thinking?"

Anna sighed. She'd gone back and forth in her thoughts on the decision for three days now, and she still didn't know the right thing to do. She had been looking forward to the adventure since receiving the letter from Fay inviting her, and she hadn't been able to stop thinking about a women's mountaineering club.

Ben cleared his throat and sat down on the bed. "Seems like you've been pretty ill the last couple of days."

"I wonder if all the fresh mountain air might do me some good. The wild flowers, the smell of glaciers coming down on the wind from higher up."

"Possibly. Or I could go by myself to send your regards and share the joyous news."

She frowned. "I can't send my husband to the meeting for female mountaineers. Preposterous."

He chuckled. "I'd never want to cross those kinds of women. I yield!"

She shook her head and gave him a playful shove. "Let me think about it for one more day. I'd very much like to go, but, of course, I want to do the best thing for our baby."

He nodded and retreated again toward the door of their bedroom.

With a sigh, Anna sipped her peppermint tea, even as her stomach turned. Being with child wasn't nearly as pleasant as she had imagined. She'd felt ill every morning of the last few days, and she hoped that wouldn't last much longer.

After a few nibbles of toast, she rose to her feet, which made the room spin a little. Once dressed, they walked toward the Gallagher house where they could all enjoy breakfast together, and she could reveal the news to everyone all at once.

Levi and Emily had already arrived when they got there. Although Anna had been disappointed to miss their surprise wedding while she had been on the mountain, she couldn't be happier for them.

"It's so wonderful to see you," Emily said, kissing her new sister-in-law on the cheek. "Greta has made the most delicious scones you'll ever eat. Can I get you some coffee?"

Anna shook her head with more of a frown than she'd meant to show, just as Greta emerged from the kitchen.

"Oh dear, you don't look well." The older woman put a fist on her hip and sized Anna up.

Her grandfather and Levi strolled in from the porch with

mugs of coffee in hand, and Ben greeted them with hearty handshakes.

"Actually," Anna said, sitting down at the dining room table. "Since everyone is here. Ben and I have some news."

"Wonderful news, in fact." Ben puffed his chest out with a grin. "We're expecting a little one."

Emily squealed and then put a hand to her mouth. "How delightful! Congratulations to both of you."

Next, her grandfather and Greta both moved in to embrace Anna.

"How are you feeling, my dear?" Greta asked.

"Not great, but I'm hoping it will pass."

"Yes, it often does, I hear," Emily chimed in. "Just a couple weeks of the nausea, perhaps."

Anna had been expecting that it would only be days, and the idea of weeks of feeling ill scared her.

Levi patted Ben on the back with a wide grin, showing the small gap in his front teeth. "Bravo, friend. What splendid news. Who would have known all those years ago on the fishing boat together that I would be uncle to your children?"

Ben laughed, then rested his hands on Anna's shoulders, which brought a calm to her. The crowded room was full of love, but it felt stifling in her current condition.

"Well, I won't make you wait a moment longer to eat. Let me go finish up, and we'll feast presently." Greta hurried back to the kitchen.

Emily touched Anna's arm. "Would you like some fresh air? We could sit on the porch for a minute before breakfast."

"That would be perfect."

It was such a pleasure to spend time with Emily again and have her become part of the family. Her friend looked so happy and light on her feet—not weighed down with the pressures she had always put on herself. She wore a light-yellow dress, which might have made most women look pale and sickly, but Emily seemed to glow, radiating happiness from the inside.

Once they were situated on the porch, Anna looked up at her mountain. Even being outside in the fresh air was a treat compared to being indoors. How much better would it be to wander through fields and rivers and spend a few evenings at base camp with a warm fire? If anything smelled bad, she could simply take a quick walk in the other direction, and the scent of evergreen trees or mountain water could wash away the nausea.

"I'm overjoyed that you're with child," Emily said, sitting on the edge of her chair, back straight as a ballerina. "That will make me an aunt!"

Anna smiled. "What a wonderful family this little one will join. So many people to love him."

"You're expecting a boy?"

"I had a dream last night," she replied. "I don't know for sure, of course, but in the dream, it was a baby boy. It would be nice to name a son after my father."

"Oh yes, that would indeed. Your father would be so happy for you."

"Thank you. And if it's a girl, I could always name her after my mother." Anna smiled, looking again toward the mountain. It would be delightful to have a daughter. "But how are things going with you and Levi? Have you settled into his home comfortably?"

Emily grinned. "Oh yes. It was quite easy to move my things in because I had nothing."

She laughed, and Anna could see that she wasn't putting

herself down at all. She was just happy for the way her life had transformed.

"I didn't realize what a marvel it could be to fall in love with your best friend. Of course, our friendship is so different now as adults, but the closeness is the same. And it's such a treat to know that he loves me no matter what I do or say, and that he's always loved me just the way I am."

Anna reached for her friend's hand. "I could not be any more excited. For the both of you. I've never seen my brother happier, truly."

Emily smiled back, but then she paused as if she'd thought of something. "Have you run into Elizabeth since she's returned?"

"No, not yet. I wish to speak with her at some point. Which I know will be uncomfortable, but I do feel for her. And, of course, it had nothing to do with her. She's such a quiet thing, though. I hope she'll understand."

Greta poked her head out the door and called, "Breakfast's ready, girls!"

They sat down to feast on Swedish pancakes with berries. A large plate of ham, tomatoes, and cucumbers also graced the table.

"When are you meeting with Miss Fuller about the women's mountaineering club, Anna?" her grandfather asked.

She glanced at Ben. "Well, previously, we had decided to meet at Camp Muir next week. Not to attempt a climb at this time of year, just to enjoy the mountain air and the views while we dream up what the club will be about."

"And is that alright? Now that you're expecting, I mean?" Greta asked. "I certainly don't know. Have you been to see a doctor yet?"

"Well, no," Anna said, twisting the napkin in her hands,

then brushing it flat on her lap. "Should I see a doctor? I thought that wasn't needed until my confinement later on. Ben and I think it would be fine, as long as I'm feeling up for it."

Ben cleared his throat and set down his fork. "She's been quite sick, actually. But we have a notion that the fresh air might do her some good. Plus, we'll be there together, so we can always turn back if things don't go well."

Anna put her hand on Ben's leg, and he looked over and winked. It sounded as if he had made up his mind that they both should go, and relief flooded over her. It was comforting to have his unwavering support.

"Well, if there's anything we can do, please let me know," Emily said. "Except, I'm not great with dogs."

Greta laughed. "Comma is always welcome with us."

After the meal, Anna hugged everyone in her family tightly before walking hand in hand with Ben to their own house. It had been a beautiful afternoon, and the weather was lovely.

"So, you think it's alright?" she asked, looking up into his brown eyes.

"Certainly. Though Greta might be right about seeing a doctor first. I know it's not needed yet, but maybe he can give some advice on the sickness you've been having. And also share his thoughts about the strenuous nature of hiking for a few days. But as long as we take it nice and easy, I have an inkling that it'll do you good."

She looked up toward the mountain, ill at ease with the idea of getting the approval of a doctor. But she forced a smile as she put her hand on her still-flat stomach.

Surely, the joy would come as the baby grew. And if it didn't, she could sort through her emotions then.

# CHAPTER FIVE
## HOSPITAL FOR THE INSANE

*Elizabeth | October 1891*

Late on a Saturday evening, after everyone else had gone to sleep, Elizabeth poured water over the coals in the cookstove for the second time. That familiar wave of dread hit her as the hiss of steam met her face, and she froze. When she looked up, the line between the wall and the ceiling seemed to tilt, and her mouth went dry and sour. It was as if the whole world shifted.

There was no particular reason for her to feel this way, which somehow made it all the worse.

An itch she couldn't scratch, like ants on her skin, plagued her, but when she looked, she saw nothing. The sensation lay below the skin, coursing through her, and no amount of scratching or rubbing could fix it—this she knew.

She glanced around to make sure she was alone, and then

with a nonchalant movement, ran one finger lightly over the copper. It was still warm but certainly held no risk of a fire starting when she walked out of the kitchen.

But this evening felt like bad luck—like icy dread seeping up her arms.

Which was more important: to follow in the footsteps of her hero Florence Nightingale and become a nurse, or to create a life so secretive and lonely that no one would institutionalize her like her old neighbor, Mrs. Hampton?

The two raged at odds with each other. To be a nurse, she had to be thought of as competent enough to take care of the injured. Or to assist mothers while they birthed their children. It was a virtue for a nurse to be meticulous and prioritize cleanliness and order.

But in Elizabeth's mind, those things took on a different meaning. They became exaggerated, and the obsessing knew no end. If she could get a handle on her thoughts, learn to control her nerves, she just might be the best nurse that ever was.

As she climbed the steps to her bedroom, her mind flashed back to the day she'd first brought up the idea of becoming a nurse with her mother. Elizabeth had always been timid about it, but after receiving high marks on a science test in high school, she'd got up the courage to broach the subject.

The blood pumping through her heart had actually made her chest ache—the anxiety had been palpable. She'd been almost too scared to say the words out loud, but she had to put it out there.

"I would love to be a nurse one day," she had said, swallowing hard. And as soon as she'd said the words, the familiar gnawing of self-doubt had crawled through her insides.

She'd prepared herself for the worst, but her mother's face had lit up.

"Excellent! Yes, I could see that. Indeed. Your marks at school are certainly promising. Perhaps you can visit your Aunt Rose Marie this summer to assist her during and after her birth. Lord knows she could use the help."

Elizabeth's chest had filled with warmth at her mother addressing her as if she were a grown woman, thinking that being a nurse was a completely reasonable dream. And that had been the start of many visits to be with her aunt for childbirth. Often, her other children had caught illnesses during those times, and Elizabeth had been able to nurse them as well. Even tending to their scrapes and injuries had kept her busy and given her valuable experience.

Now that she was almost eighteen years old, and no longer courting, the time had come to pursue this. She would find out soon if she could follow along with their family's doctor when he did his rounds with the families that lived outside of town. If that went well, she could ask him for a letter of recommendation. With that, the hospital might let her volunteer or even apply for a student nurse apprenticeship.

As she slipped under the covers and closed her eyes, she felt as if death were settling upon her, but she knew not to trust that feeling of weight pressing down on her chest. Everything would be better in the morning.

❧

A FEW DAYS LATER, her father arranged a meeting with Dr. Glazier so Elizabeth could ask him about joining him occasionally on house calls.

Her brother was sitting at the dining room table writing

when she came down the stairs, fully dressed in her best and ready to ask the doctor for the favor. Her mother stood at the cookstove frying pork fat.

Elizabeth wore a mint green dress with mother-of-pearl buttons going down the back. The white sash wrapped around her waist and tied behind her in a bow that made her backside look bigger than it was.

She mustered a confident smile and smoothed her dress. "Are you wishing me luck even as you ignore me?"

James chuckled, then looked up from the letter he was writing, tapping his pen in the ink. "I need to stay busy if I'm going to write anything worthwhile today," he said.

He wrote for the Seattle Post-Intelligencer. With the same green eyes and dark hair as their father, he looked nothing like his fair-haired, blue-eyed sister.

"Plus, it's Dr. Glazier, isn't it? He's known our family since we were small children. I'm sure he'll allow it."

She exhaled shakily and nodded.

"Breakfast smells delicious, dear," her father said, thumping down the stairs in his finest suit. Then he focused his gaze on Elizabeth. "If he says yes, when would you begin?"

"Probably right away." She grinned, imagining herself in a smart walking suit—visiting families with a proper doctor and her as the student nurse, at least in their eyes.

"Well, after we eat, I'm off to drop this wheat at the store, and then I have to pick up another shipment from the docks," her father said.

Grayson's Grocer was doing well, and she was proud of her father and their family business.

"It will be an honor if he says yes, Elizabeth."

"Thanks, Father," she said, beaming.

He was the hardest one to make proud, but she knew he

loved the idea of her helping others. She wasn't confident the doctor would say yes, though.

Just as the doorbell knocker sounded, the image of her burning candle from her bedroom flashed in her mind. She was pretty sure she'd blown it out, but after all the conversation, it was hard to tease that memory out from all the other mornings of blowing out the flame.

She shouldn't check it. Doing so made her doubting worse in the long run. Plus, it would be rude not to greet the doctor right away, as he knew she was the one who wished to speak with him.

But the image of her bedroom candle wouldn't leave her mind, along with the skirt she had decided not to wear and tossed onto her chest of drawers. Hopefully, it was well out of reach of that flame, assuming she'd forgotten to blow it out after all.

And then, every logical sense drained out of her as the nerves took over. She bounded up the stairs as quickly as she could to make sure all was well. When she crossed the threshold into her bedroom, she froze. Everything was exactly in its place, and it relieved her agony to see the unlit candle. But she knew that as soon as she tore her eyes away from the sight, the nerves would return. After a few minutes, she made herself turn and then raced back down as the doctor was checking his pocket watch.

"There she is. Hello, Miss Grayson," he said, taking off his hat with a small bow. "What can I help you with, my dear?"

"Would you like to join us for breakfast, sir?" she asked, nearly out of breath.

"It smells divine, but I'm afraid I don't have time. I'm sorry to be rude, but it can't be helped. I could take some tea with you in the sitting room while we talk, though."

"I'll fetch the tea so that you and Elizabeth can speak right away," her mother said, disappearing into the kitchen.

The doctor nodded and lowered himself onto an overstuffed chair. "My dear, I saw you running away up the stairs just as I came in the door. Do you still suffer from your nerves? Like you did as a child?"

The tone in his voice held a note of sympathy, and Elizabeth steeled her face so as not to let it betray anything. When she was younger, before she had learned to keep her private business to herself, Dr. Glazier had treated her for some fainting spells and various "fits of madness." His words.

"I'm not sure what you mean. But I'm terribly sorry about the wait. I hope I didn't keep you waiting long." She cleared her throat. "I was wondering if perhaps I could come along with you on some of your doctor visits. I'd love to be a nurse one day."

"Ahh, I remember you mentioned that to me once before. So, you're still hoping to become a nurse then?"

She nodded.

Her mother returned with a steaming pot of tea and a plate of shortbread cookies. She bowed slightly to the doctor, which Elizabeth felt was unnecessary, then left.

Dr. Glazier picked up a cookie between his thumb and forefinger, examining it.

"Let me ask you something. When you went upstairs, were you . . . checking things?" His voice was soft with a hint of pity hovering.

She shook her head, mute.

He sighed, then looked toward the kitchen and lowered his voice. "I certainly wouldn't want you to end up in the Washington State Hospital for the Insane at Fort Steilacoom."

Heat burned her cheeks as her pulse sped up.

He exhaled so dramatically that her arms tingled with numbness. That's what happened when she felt a dizzy spell coming on, so she bit her lip to distract herself.

"I'm trying to do you a kindness, Miss Grayson," he said warily. "Marry a good young man. Start a family. Keep your home peaceful, and try not to trigger your nerves. Working as a nurse involves all kinds of unexpected situations, and I'm afraid your mind might get the better of you."

She plastered a smile on her face and poured herself a cup of hot tea. "It's alright if you don't want a student nurse following you around. I thank you for considering me anyhow."

Heart racing, she smoothed her skirts over her lap. She was sweating. With a fierce hold, she clutched her knees.

"I know you better than you think I do," he said with compassion. "Elizabeth, I've watched you grow up, and you're quite smart. I'm confident about that. But I've seen you struggle with . . . perhaps voices in your head or irrational fears—"

"I certainly do not hear voices," she replied fervently.

"Whatever the illness may be, it wouldn't do to have you in charge of the sick and injured."

He paused with a look on his features, as if he might take it all back. Time had wrinkled his face, and his eyes had always seemed wise, but now they cut into her. It had once been a strong desire of hers to impress this old man by becoming a nurse and joining the medical field.

But all those hopes came crashing down with the realization that he didn't even think she was *normal* enough to be a nurse.

# CHAPTER SIX
## ANNA'S BROWN WINDSOR SOAP

*Anna | October 1891 | The Third Month*

Greta had invited Anna, Emily, and Heather over for a day of making brown Windsor soap, Anna's favorite.

The early fall air was crisp with the smell of fallen leaves, but Anna knew that by the afternoon, the sun would shine high and the heat would be glorious. It was the kind of day where you began with a shawl and a chill but ended up sweaty and rolling up your shirt sleeves by early evening.

It would be a relief for the family bookstore to be cooler during the day while she and her grandfather worked there. The original Gallagher bookstore had been burned to the ground, and they had rented a storefront. It was a smaller place, but the views of the water and the mountain beyond were breathtaking.

Anna preferred the new location, actually. It was a joy to

be surrounded by books and the company of her grandfather on most days, and she was proud to still have her employment after marriage. She was also proud to help her grandfather with some of the more arduous tasks at the bookstore, as his strength had waned.

As she walked toward the house she grew up in, with crispy leaves underfoot, she remembered back to the fall two years prior, when she and Greta had worked so hard to provide for their family in the wake of losing a shipment of books for the bookstore.

When she arrived at the Gallagher house, a peaceful relaxation settled over her. She was home.

Greta welcomed her in with a long hug and a small pat to her belly.

"I'm just beside myself with delight," Greta said. "I bet you can't contain your excitement either."

Anna smiled while biting her lip. "Am I the first to arrive?"

"Yes, you are, but don't worry, I've got everything handled. You just take a seat and rest."

"That would be silly. I'm not tired. Rather, I'm exhilarated from my walk here and happy to help."

She didn't need people to treat her differently already. Sure, she might need to step outside now and then, but that was something she could take care of herself.

"You have all the ingredients for the soap?" she asked, reaching for a spare apron just like old times.

Greta put her hand out and listed things with her fingers. "I've got the ashes, rain water, lard, bergamot, cloves, and . . . What am I forgetting?"

"Cinnamon," Anna replied with a smile.

"Of course." Greta clapped her hands together. "We

should open the windows now to get some fresh air circulating."

Anna couldn't agree more. She moved toward the kitchen windows and opened them wide. A gust of delicious-smelling wind greeted her and brushed the curtains aside.

As Greta went to the living room to open windows, she heard a tapping at the front door, followed by Emily peeking her head inside.

"You don't need to knock. You're family!" Anna said, going to give her friend an embrace.

Emily blushed. "I think I'll be knocking for a little while longer. But I appreciate the sentiment."

Heather arrived moments later, and the room filled with soft chatter and greetings. Anna was so glad that Heather was close enough that they could spend afternoons together anytime they wanted to. Pisha reached for Anna's hand, and she bent down to greet the girl.

"I'm so glad that you've joined us for the afternoon," Anna said in a sweet voice. "Can you help me grate the cinnamon?"

Pisha lifted her eyebrows in surprised excitement, in the endearing way that little girls do. Anna squeezed the girl's hand and led her to the kitchen. She certainly wouldn't mind having a sweet little girl like Pisha.

But what if she had a boy, and he turned out as mean as Peter?

Or condescending like Connor?

She wondered what the mothers of those boys were like. Perhaps they also weren't thrilled with the timing of their pregnancies and how life changed for them.

Emily joined her in the kitchen. "You're going to be an exemplary mother, Anna. I can't wait until my time comes.

How many months were you married before you knew you were with child?"

Anna swallowed. "I suppose seven or eight."

*Too soon.*

"Ahh, that sounds about right. Although I hope it's a little sooner for me. Wouldn't that be fun to have children the same age?"

That idea made Anna smile. What she wouldn't have given to have a cousin in her life just exactly her age. She loved how close she was with her family and how they continued to grow and expand.

Once they had everything they needed assembled, they got to work. Greta had been saving ashes from the right kind of wood. The ash from pinewood and Douglas firs wouldn't do at all for making lye. She'd been keeping it all in a covered bucket that she now brought in from the back deck.

"Perhaps you should take Pisha outside to play while we make the lye," Greta said to Anna.

She frowned, but Greta was quick to defend the request.

"Well, we can't have her out there all alone. She'll get bored. She loves playing with you. And you know it can be a little dangerous—"

"Fine, I understand," she replied. "Come on, Pisha. Let's play a game under the cherry tree."

"Okay!" the girl said enthusiastically.

Outside, a cool breeze and fresh air greeted them.

"How do you like living in town? With your father?" she asked the girl.

"I like it. I'm happy."

That was a relief, as well as a whole different experience for Heather than for her daughter. Anna was glad Pisha wasn't feeling much of the fear and uncertainty her mother was.

"I've heard that you made friends. Tell me about them."

"Mary is my friend. We play dolls," the girl replied shyly.

"She sounds wonderful. I used to love playing dolls with my friends when I was a girl."

Anna sighed. She imagined what the ladies were doing inside without her. First, they would put the ashes into an iron pot and then add rainwater that Greta had collected in a barrel. They would then boil the mixture until most of the ashes had settled to the bottom.

Greta would skim the lye from the top of that boiling concoction, careful as ever not to get any on her skin. The fumes alone seemed dangerous, but Anna had only heard stories of how costly a mistake with lye could be.

That liquid, skimmed from the top, would be boiled down even further while the others warmed leftover cooking lard and prepared the spices that would make the beloved brown Windsor soap. When it was all combined—lye, lard, cinnamon, bergamot, and cloves—the final product would be a special treat. It wouldn't be quite like the fancy stuff that came from England, but it was lovely just as they made it.

Anna smiled at Pisha as they spent time under the cherry tree making daisy chains and trying to whistle with blades of grass until, finally, Greta called for them.

Inside, the smells were so strong that Anna was grateful she had missed some of it. She loved the wonderful scents of brown Windsor soap, but her stomach wasn't as tough as it used to be.

As Greta poured the steaming concoction into the mold, Anna marveled at the creamy liquid she would enjoy in her baths in the coming months. They would each get five bars, but it would have to cure for about a month first.

Heather sat down next to her. "I wanted to tell you I'll be

visiting the reservation around the end of April. I know that's when you're expecting your child."

Anna's heart sank. Was her friend planning to leave for the birth? Her only friend who knew how those things happened?

"Oh, well, that—"

"I fully plan to be here for the birth, though. That's what I was trying to say. I'll stay until you have your baby. Then I'll leave." She paused. "I was invited to come at that time . . . by my mother."

"What?" Anna asked in surprise. She'd thought Heather's mother was dead.

Greta drew closer, waiting for Heather to say more.

"Yes, I wrote to her after my grandmother died. She lives on the Suquamish reservation that I visit, but she has always refused to see me. I thought she should know about her mother."

"Did she write back?" Anna asked.

"No. Actually, it was my cousin Lana. She wrote back on my mother's behalf. And they'd like me to come at the end of April."

"That's wonderful," Anna said. "I'm so glad to hear about your mother. Do you think she wants to reconcile?"

"I'm unsure, but her inviting me is a good sign. But don't worry, I won't leave until after your birth."

Relief filled Anna, and she reached her hand toward her friend's arm. "You're too good to me. I don't even know if I could do it without you."

"You could. But I want to be there for it. For you."

"Thank you," she said. Then she turned to Pisha, who was on the floor near the fire, playing with the cat. "Are you excited to visit your family on the reservation?"

The girl shrugged and went back to her play.

Heather's lips drew into a hard line, and Anna could sense the tension.

"It's been a few months since she was there last," she said, trying to put her friend at ease. "It's probably hard for her to remember the details at her age."

"Perhaps. But I worry that she'll one day prefer town living to that of her own people."

Anna nodded with a frown. "How long will you stay for this trip?"

"A few weeks. Maybe a month."

With Heather leaving right after the birth, it made her nervous for the lying-in days after she'd have her child. What did one do all day with an infant? She felt uneasy at the prospect of being alone to figure it out.

Emily took off her apron and sat down at the table with them. "It smells divine in here. What are you all talking about? Am I interrupting?"

She must have sensed the somberness in the air.

"Oh, I'm just thinking about my lying-in after the birth. And how I'm so grateful Heather will be there for the birthing."

"I plan to bring over meals as often as I can," Emily said. "And I can come take Comma for walks. I know little about babies, but I remember helping to take care of my sister, Lauren, when she was small. I'll do whatever I can to help."

"Thank you," Anna said with a smile. She knew Emily would do her best to be there for her, but the fact that Heather would have somewhere else to be put a rock in the pit of her stomach.

# CHAPTER SEVEN
## GRINDING STONE

*Elizabeth*

After the doctor left, Elizabeth walked into the dining room with blurred vision from her tears. James looked up with wide eyes and put his pen down—for once. Behind him, their mother prepared a tin pail of food.

"What happened?" James asked, standing.

Before Elizabeth could answer, her mother spoke without looking up. "Your father forgot his lunch. Could one of you walk over there and give it to him? He's got such a busy day today."

Elizabeth wiped her face and nodded, waving her hand dismissively at her brother. "I can."

"Thank you, dear," her mother said, finally looking up. "Oh my, are you alright? I'm sorry I forgot to ask. How did it go with the doctor?"

"Not well, but that's all right." She smiled with feigned confidence. "Perhaps I can apply straightaway for being a student nurse at the hospital."

"Of course. Yes, that's true. Head up, dear." Her mother stood, handing her the lunch.

She was aware of her brother's eyes on her, but she couldn't look at him just yet or her smile would waver.

Once their mother had hurried out to the clothesline, James turned to her and leaned forward. "What *really* happened?"

Elizabeth recounted the words that had made her ill.

James scoffed. "I always knew he was a grumpy old man."

She bit the inside of her cheek, and the weight of two major rejections in such a short period weighed heavily upon her. First Levi and now this.

James shrugged. "He's getting quite old, anyway. Perhaps he simply doesn't want such a young nurse there, making him look incompetent."

She laughed despite her general air of humiliation, then walked toward the door to don her shawl.

Ever since she was a little girl, Grayson's Grocer had been a fun place to visit. She used to spend time in the back rooms, playing amongst the overflow of stock—barrels of flour, piles of fabrics. As long as she didn't make a mess, she was welcome to create any imaginary world she desired.

As an adult, it wasn't as fun but still a comforting place to be.

She strolled toward the store, mulling over the conversation with the doctor. He wasn't trying to be cruel, which made his sentiments all the more upsetting.

Why had she ever opened up to him about the things she'd struggled with when she was younger?

Even her parents had seemed to forget them, or at least expected that she had grown out of them. It would be best if everyone believed that.

When she arrived at her father's store, his eyes lit up to see her. He waved before disappearing into the back room.

As soon as she set her hands on the counter of the store, it seemed to sway beneath her. It must be a dizzy spell coming over her.

She pressed both her palms to the surface to stabilize herself, closed her eyes, and tried to relax her shoulders.

But then the very earth seemed to shudder beneath her. The floor lifted her and then rolled back down, nearly toppling her.

A crash sounded behind her as something fell to the floor, and her father came stumbling from the back room.

"Earthquake!" he shouted. "Everyone outside—now!"

He ushered two customers outside, then ran to the back room to get his store clerk, who had just gone in there.

When Elizabeth turned back toward the door, a box of supplies fell off a shelf above the panel. A series of thuds sounded as sacks of sugar flew out of the wooden box.

A small old woman screamed while another darted out the door as soon as there was a break in the rumbling.

The old woman froze, staring up at the shelves above, so Elizabeth rushed toward her as quickly as she could while the ground beneath her continued to shudder.

As she wrapped one arm around the woman's waist, she felt the weight of something hit the back of her head. A box crashed to the floor next to them, and steel pots spilled out, making a great clanging sound.

With her head throbbing, she nearly dragged the woman out the door as the ground continued to roll. Outside, people poured out of buildings where boards of awnings were splintering and stone was cracked. Some looked terrified, but others seemed only to be flustered.

The smell of spilled wine and milk from the grocer mixed in a tangy aroma—there would be a big mess to clean up after this. Across the street, a team of horses reared and nearly trampled a young lady with a straw hat before an older lady yanked her arm hard to pull her out of the way.

Just as Elizabeth heard grinding stone below her feet, the movement stopped. Everything was still for a moment before people jumped to their feet. She looked around, surveying the damage and the mess. The whole thing had started in what she'd thought to be a fit of panic. But the world hadn't just *seemed* off-kilter—it truly had been.

Supplies that had fallen from shelves cluttered the floor of the store, but the building itself was intact.

A little boy nearby sat alone, crying out, so Elizabeth hurried over to him.

He had a dark red gash in his leg. She ran back into the grocer as her father and the clerk were rushing out.

She reached for the bandages behind the counter and went back to the little boy.

He looked up at her with a flustered look on his face. Blood already stained the bottom of his shorts, and he tried to wipe at the redness dripping onto the wood-planked walkway.

"Here, let me get this bandaged up," she said soothingly. Pulling out some gauze and alcohol to wipe the blood away, she cleaned the wound first. It was fairly deep, but the bleeding was already slowing, which was a good sign.

"Thank you, miss," he said, taking a shaky breath and sitting back against the building in relief.

Once she had him cleaned and bandaged, she walked toward her father, but someone approached her from behind.

It was the woman who had pulled the young lady away from the horses. She had saved her from being trampled, but now the girl was crying hysterically and holding onto her arm.

"I'm sorry to bother you, miss, but I thought you might help my daughter as well. I'm not sure what's wrong with her arm."

"It hurts bad. I think it's broken," the girl said between whimpers.

Elizabeth knew there was no way it was broken from her mother pulling her to safety by yanking her wrist. But perhaps she had fallen after that.

"Where exactly does it hurt? Did you fall in the commotion?" she asked the girl, who wasn't much younger than herself.

"It's just radiating up and down my arm. But no, I didn't fall."

*Probably her elbow pulled out of socket.*

Her cousin had had this happen a few times, and their doctor in Oregon had shown her how to fix it so they wouldn't have to keep fetching him.

Elizabeth placed her hand on the girl's wrist with a soft touch. She pressed on the bones of her fingers, then carefully moved up the girl's arm as she winced. "May I try something?"

The girl nodded meekly, so Elizabeth positioned herself behind her, putting two fingers in the crook of the girl's elbow. She slowly brought the girl's arm up, her hand bent to the side, bringing it to her shoulder. The closeness to another person's face made her blush, but she pushed away the feeling to focus on the task at hand.

"No, stop. It hurts!"

"Will you trust me?" Elizabeth gave her best serious face, and the girl nodded doubtfully.

She directed her hand the rest of the way, then felt the small snap in her inner elbow. The girl's face tightened for a moment, then relaxed.

"Oh my! It feels better." She rested against her mother with a relieved grin.

"Thank you so much, miss," the mother said before leading her daughter away.

Elizabeth smiled politely and then looked up to see a crowd around them. Her heart was pounding, and she wiped the dampness of her palms on her dusty skirts.

"She bandaged me up too," the little boy said, showing off his leg to the onlookers.

She glanced around and met her father's gaze. With raised eyebrows, an admiring smile grew on his face. He nodded at her with a proud look in his eye.

"Yes, very well done," he said, huffing as he walked toward the group.

Her chest was light with happiness that she could use her skills in a crisis, not to mention how calm she had been. She'd always wondered how she might act in a grave moment—if she'd be able to keep her head and do what needed to be done.

It was too bad Dr. Glazier hadn't been there to see it.

It had been easy, as if time had slowed considerably. There had been time enough for everything that needed to happen, and it had been an advantage that her mind could work at lightning speeds.

The crowd dispersed, slowly at first, while chatting about the ordeal. With a bounce in her gait, Elizabeth moved toward the mess of the store when she realized her head was still throbbing. She'd forgotten about the box landing on her. With a finger, she reached up to touch her hair, but there was no moisture. When she looked down at her hand, she only saw the dried blood from the boy's wound.

Blood also smeared the walkway where he had been, and she reached for a rag from the counter to go back outside and wipe it up.

*Would it stain the wood permanently?*

It didn't matter all that much. There were all manners of stains and spots on both the street and the wooden walkways. But her mind fixated on how ghastly a blood stain would be outside a grocer.

All at once, her stomach turned, and she felt ill. She sat down and leaned her back against the store wall, and her father strode toward her.

"Easy there," he said gently. "I saw that box fall on you. You might feel out of sorts for a spell. Don't you worry about this mess. I'll get it all taken care of. Let's get you home."

"I'm alright. Dizzy." She looked up at her father looming above her with the bright sky surrounding the outline of his frame. He was proud of her, and the satisfaction of that achievement buoyed her.

He nodded and sat down on the ground with her. The clerk went back inside and picked up a broom.

Despite her relief and even joy, the street in front of her kept spinning in waves. Even so, she still reveled in her moment. She had helped people, and it felt great. The small crowd had looked at her with admiration. A smile spread over her face as she leaned her pounding head against her father's shoulder.

Then her eyes returned to the blood smear on the ground, and she hoped she had bandaged the boy up correctly.

What if the wound ended up getting infected because she had been careless?

And perhaps she ought to dump a bucket of water over the walkway to dilute the blood's power. She looked down at the dried blood on her fingers. She tried to wipe it off on her skirts, but the crimson stains remained.

Her pulse quickened, even more so than during the earthquake. It was as if her brain was warning her of some danger another part of her knew was no threat at all. Without being able to reconcile the two feelings, she closed her eyes and rested her head against the wall of the store.

*I helped people today.*

*I did everything right.*

*It doesn't matter that there is still dried blood on my fingers.*

# CHAPTER EIGHT
## FRESH AIR AND WILDFLOWERS

*Anna*

Anna slammed the front door hard as she and Ben returned from the doctor. No surprise that his advice had been old-fashioned, but it still stung.

"He didn't mean to offend you," Ben said, hanging his hat on the hook by the door.

Anna surveyed the books on the floor. They had surely fallen off their shelves in the earthquake. The timing had been eerie—just as they were about to meet with the doctor who gave horrid advice, the whole earth shuddered.

She whirled around to face him. "Don't tell me you're taking his side on this—"

"I would never," he said with a calming smile.

"According to him, elevation and strenuous exercise would prevent fertility, and we clearly know that's not the case. I think we very well might have conceived this baby in the exact place we're going."

He stopped with a lopsided grin. "That was a glorious night."

"So he's wrong on that point. How can we trust his advice on the other things?"

Ben put his arms around her, and she relaxed. She knew the doctor was wrong, but his scowls and groans of disapproval bothered her.

"I think we'll find you a new doctor." He looked down at her with a thoughtful expression. "Someone more . . . forward-thinking. But we'll do that as soon as we return."

A smile grew on her face, and her heart lifted. "Yes?"

"Yes, let's go. The worst that can happen is you get too fatigued, and understandably so. Or that the nausea prevents you from enjoying the trip. If so, we can turn right back around and send Miss Fuller your regards. I'm sure she'd be willing to meet up with you in Yelm or Tacoma another time."

"And what of his thoughts on my sickness?" Her eyes were filling with tears.

"He's wrong. Our little one knows you want him."

"I don't see how that could even be possible, anyway—nausea and vomiting because you're subconsciously trying to reject the baby? He sounds positively mad. Do people believe these things?"

Ben shrugged and reached for the closest books on the floor. "Don't pay him any mind. Like I said, we'll find a new doctor when we return from the mountain."

She breathed a sigh of relief and began to help tidy up. Even though the doctor's beliefs about her sickness were clearly wrong, it was good to hear Ben say it out loud.

"After we're finished, I'll go pack. This will be a wonderful trip."

When the room was righted, she kissed her husband and hurried up the stairs. If she never saw that foolish doctor again, that would suit her just fine. She'd be better off getting advice of this nature from Heather, or someone else who at least had the experience of being with child.

Even Elizabeth Grayson probably knew more, as she had attended many of the births of her aunt. And that thought reminded her she needed to write the girl. Even though her presence had always been odd and too quiet, she was a good person, and Anna wanted to make sure she knew they could remain friends despite things not working out with her brother.

Once she had changed into her linen nightgown, she lit a candle and set it on her desk to write. She loved the stationery her grandfather and Greta had given her for the wedding. It had come along with the dark brown desk her grandfather had made himself. It was the stationery from their store that she'd always envied—thick creamy paper, the whitest she'd ever seen, with a stamp of wild flowers at the top. She put her pen to the beautiful sheet to write.

*Dear Elizabeth,*

*By now, you are surely far past any concerns about my brother or the time he spent courting you. But I wanted to let you know I consider you a friend always. I hope I can see you again soon, if you'll have me, and if it wouldn't be too uncomfortable for you. Levi has loved Emily since we were in primary school, and the death of her husband was such a shock to us all. The orchestration of events was something that no one could have believed was going to happen a year ago. Please write to me soon, and let me know if you'd like me to visit sometime.*

*Your friend,*
*Anna Chambers*

She folded the paper gingerly and slid it into the crisp white envelope. Next, she held the wax spoon over the candle until the gold wax melted, then she poured it onto the envelope. Quickly, she stamped it with the likeness of the mountain. She was sure that Greta had special-ordered the bronze stamp, and she couldn't love it any more than she did.

❧

THE TRAIN WHISTLE SHRIEKED, and Anna peered out the window at the city covered in fog. The early morning always inspired her to get outside, but today was special. In just a few days' time, they would arrive at base camp to meet with Fay.

Every smell on the train bombarded her: leather boots with mud caked on them, sweaty cotton, the aged cheese someone had in a paper bag. She longed to arrive in Yelm as quickly as possible.

She had the handkerchief Greta had given her. It had been soaked in the essence of mint and dried in the sun, and now she discreetly held it over her nose whenever she needed a respite from the maddening scents that tried their best to make her stomach revolt.

"A beautiful day for a train ride," Ben said, putting his arm around her.

With a quick smile, she glanced up at him and then laid her head on his shoulder. Her eyes were heavy with fatigue, and it would be good to rest while she could.

By the time they arrived in Yelm, her stomach was furious. A combination of the quick movement, horrid smells, and no fresh air had created the perfect disaster. She took only a few steps from the train pedestal and emptied her stomach into the dust.

Ben stood in front of her, facing the other way, attempting to block the scene.

When she finished, he offered his arm. "Nearly every man gets sick on the open seas. I suppose being with child is a voyage in itself."

Her knees were weak, but she nodded in agreement, then started walking.

They weren't in need of an entire group or team this time, but John had offered to join them. So, it would be the three of them to journey from Yelm to the Camp of the Clouds. It was possible that they'd see Fay in Yelm or on the path there, but they hadn't coordinated those details, so she wasn't sure how it would play out.

When they arrived at their rendezvous location, John had already set up camp. He had pitched his tent near the large tree that Anna loved, and he stoked the blazing fire. The weather was cooler now, so the warmth of the flames was a welcome respite.

A crisp wind blew through the field, and she finally relaxed.

"Great to see you both," John said, standing as they arrived. "It'll be nice to make the trip when it's not hotter than blazes, won't it?"

"That it will," Ben replied, setting down their bags near the fire.

"And congratulations to both of you," John said, nodding to Anna and reaching his hand to shake Ben's.

"Thank you," she said, genuinely glad to see him.

She lowered herself down on the dirt to unpack their dinner while Ben set their tent up.

"When do you expect the baby?" John asked.

Ben grinned while he shook out the canvas of the tent. "End of April or thereabouts."

"A baby in the spring. Darn poetic is what that is," John said, shaking his head with a smile.

"And the father-to-be is a poet himself," Anna said, winking at Ben.

"Oh, I wouldn't go that far. I do enjoy a clever poem, and if I feel one floating around inside, I'll let it out on paper as a courtesy," he replied.

"You're being modest." She turned to John. "Shall I heat some chicken for our dinner, or do you already have something in mind?"

"Much obliged. Chicken sounds great. I have some grits and ham for the morning I can share."

Anna had also packed bread, cheese, and apples she'd picked from her grandfather's trees. It should last the entire trip, and they wouldn't need to eat any tack like they would've if they'd been going to a higher elevation than base camp.

She also had a stash of dried mint leaves to make tea if needed.

The next morning, they packed their things, and John went into the small town to hire mules. The plan was for Anna to walk for as long as she felt comfortable, and then in the afternoon, or whenever fatigue came, they would transfer the supplies from one mule to the bags of the men, then she would ride.

This made her feel like a burden before they had even set out on the trail. But both John and Ben assured her they didn't mind, and that they could always make camp early if they all agreed on it. Fay planned to be at base camp for a few days beyond their meeting time, so if they were a day or two late, it would be no trouble.

The first hours of the day were crisp and sunny—a perfect fall day. The smells were divine, and her nausea was lifted by noon. Seeing how she felt great, she didn't think it was necessary to ride a mule that day. Ben agreed, as long as they could make camp in the early afternoon.

But after a good night's rest, Anna awoke more nauseated than ever. She wasn't sure if it was because of the previous day's exertion or not getting enough to eat and drink throughout the day, which had become more important than ever in how her body handled the journey.

She began the morning walking and hoping more than anything that the sickness would lift so she could enjoy the rest of the trip to the beautiful fields of wildflowers at the camping place near the base of the mountain. It was called Paradise.

# CHAPTER NINE
## THE PAINTING

*Elizabeth*

A knock at the door broke the early afternoon silence. Elizabeth set down her cup of tea and the medical journal she was studying.

She smoothed her dress as she walked toward the oak door she rarely enjoyed answering.

When she cracked it open, she saw the man from the train —Mr. Bailey.

"Good afternoon, Miss Grayson. Is your brother at home?" He took off his hat and looked past her into the living room.

"Oh. No, he's off on a writing assignment. He should return by dinner, though. Shall I give him a message for you?"

He seemed as if he was thinking about that for a minute. She watched his gaze dart around his well-shined leather shoes covered in beads of late September rain. He was well-dressed and probably much too hot in his suit, but his tie lay ever so neatly loose against his neck.

When she realized she had been scrutinizing Mr. Bailey so closely, she looked up into his eyes with alarm.

But his gaze was still down on his shoes, which put her at ease.

Her mother came from behind her. "Where are your manners, Elizabeth? Invite the man indoors and offer some tea."

She could feel her face flushing. He was here to see her brother, not for afternoon tea.

"That's alright, ma'am," Mr. Bailey said, putting his hat back on. "I'll try again tomorrow evening."

Then he pivoted and walked away, his smart heels clicking against the cobblestone.

"Well, I'll be," her mother said with a hand on her hip. "Did you even catch his name? He's a handsome fellow."

"That's North Bailey."

The encounter confirmed for Elizabeth that she hadn't made a friend out of Mr. Bailey on the train. Nevertheless, he wanted to get in touch with her brother. This, of course, was for the best. Even though he was handsome, as her mother suggested, the last thing she needed was a man to be distracted with, even, and especially, one who took no interest in her.

The following evening, a knock at the door sounded just as they were about to sit down to eat dinner.

"That must be Mr. Bailey," her mother said to James. "You must invite him to stay for the meal."

James went to the door and greeted Mr. Bailey heartily. After a moment of low voices, both men returned to the dining room.

"He'd be delighted to stay for dinner, Ma."

"Wonderful. I've got a seat right here for you next to James. We were expecting you, of course."

"Thank you for the kind offer, Mrs. Grayson. Much appreciated." Mr. Bailey gave a small bow toward her and then glanced at Elizabeth. "Evening, Miss Grayson."

She nodded and then looked down at her hands awkwardly.

Why was her tongue always tied when she most wanted to speak?

She might have greeted him, since she already knew him in a small way. Or she could have welcomed him to the table, but instead she lowered her eyes, blushing and wondering if he still didn't like her.

James and Mr. Bailey sat and the meal began. They passed around platters of sliced duck and scalloped potatoes until everyone had full plates. Elizabeth knew her mother had planned a fancy meal in anticipation of a dinner guest. Lit candles adorned the polished wood table, along with mint leaves from the garden at each place setting.

Mr. Grayson cleared his throat. "So, James tells us you're a train conductor."

Mr. Bailey's face lit up. "Yes, sir. For about five years now. But on the days I don't have trains scheduled, I actually do a lot of farming. Tomatoes are my specialty."

"Now, I can't seem to get my tomatoes to grow around here," Mrs. Grayson said with a frown. "Do tell me how you do it."

"I'd be happy to come by in early spring and help you plant some of my very own seeds."

"Why, that would be fantastic." Mrs. Grayson beamed.

"Indeed," Mr. Grayson said with a friendly air. He put

extra butter on his serving of scalloped potatoes. "You should come by our grocer sometime, and I'll find the perfect bottle of wine for you. That earthquake knocked quite a few good bottles onto the ground, but we just got a new shipment today."

"I will do that. Thank you, sir." He paused and then decided to add, "I hope your store didn't take too much damage in the quake."

Mr. Grayson nodded as he wiped his mouth with a crisp napkin. "Thank you kindly. We've got everything cleaned up and restored."

Toward the end of the meal, Mrs. Grayson invited him to stay for dessert and coffee.

"I've made a pumpkin pie that always wins the baking competitions. It simply can't be beat."

"Unfortunately, I can't stay much longer this evening," he said, standing to his feet as soon as the last person had finished their plate. "It was a pleasure to dine with you fine folks."

"Thanks for joining us, Mr. Bailey." Elizabeth's father stood and patted the man on his back. "Perhaps we can get a slice of pie wrapped up for you to take along."

"I'll get right on that." Mrs. Grayson disappeared into the kitchen.

"Can I have a quick gentleman's word?" Mr. Bailey said quietly to James.

"Of course," he replied, standing and buttoning his vest.

The men excused themselves to the living room.

Elizabeth didn't feel much like pie herself, so she wandered down the hall toward the foyer. Perhaps after Mr. Bailey left, her brother might accompany her on an evening walk for some fresh air, which always calmed her nerves.

She examined the paintings near the front door. She'd

always loved the one with a deep blue whale in frothy water. Another was of purple and yellow flowers against a crisp mountain backdrop.

A voice from behind her startled the serenity.

"They're beautiful."

It was Mr. Bailey, his hat in hand.

"Oh, hello." She didn't know what else to say.

In her mind, she watched herself comment on his reading habits on the train, followed by his face changing—his whole countenance shifting.

She pulled a strand of her hair out of her face and behind her ear. His gaze tracked the movement of her hand, and then he looked back into her eyes with a kind expression, which made her shoulders relax.

"You have pretty hair," he said, maintaining eye contact.

Her mouth opened slightly in surprise. She knew there was no hope of saying anything intelligible, so she snapped it shut again.

"You're difficult to read, Miss Grayson. Usually, I can read people quite well. But I haven't quite figured you out."

With everything inside her, Elizabeth wanted to come up with a witty remark—to banter playfully with this man. His closeness and charming smile made her pulse race.

"I'm sorry. I've made you uncomfortable," he said, biting his lip.

She shook her head. "No, it's me. I make everything uncomfortable."

He laughed. "Well, let's put you at ease then, shall we? Tell me about this painting here. The one with the blue whale."

They both turned toward the wall, and she felt relief when his gaze was off of her. "A local artist painted it. My father acquired it shortly after I was born. I've seen it my whole life."

"And you like it?"

"I didn't at first. When I was a girl, the whale seemed angry, and sometimes it would be in my dreams. But as I got older, I came to see that it's actually the waves that are angry. The whale is just trying to survive. Look at his eyes."

"Hmm, I see," he said, stealing a glance at her, which she caught out of the corner of her eye.

They stood a moment longer before they both turned back toward the door at the same time. Her shoulder brushed up against his arm, and butterflies pinged around her stomach at the touch.

His peaceful presence had slowly put her at ease. Even so, he had called her pretty—well, her hair.

"Do you know why I came here, Miss Grayson?"

She shook her head without a word, not wanting to say anything she might regret.

"I'd like to take you on a walk tomorrow. Your brother has agreed to join us. What do you say?"

"Are you sure?" She cleared her throat. "I mean, yes, if you like. That would be lovely."

He put on his hat and flashed a smile. "Yes. I'd like it very much."

She studied his face, and that's when she noticed the way he was looking at her. Finally, she saw his look of delight.

He was interested in her. And perhaps not just for discussing fine art.

As he walked out the door, she pressed her lips together in thought. The exhilaration of being the center of his attention made her dizzy, but not in a bad way. He must not have been bothered by her previous comment on the train, and now he would *very much* like to take her on a walk?

The prospect was both enchanting and terrifying.

# CHAPTER TEN
## A BEAUTIFULLY LAYERED EXPERIENCE

*Anna*

The previous two days of walking and riding mules toward base camp had been difficult for Anna to bear. There had been moments of bliss. But most of the time she'd been concentrating on not expressing the contents of her stomach, which felt particularly undignified when there was nowhere to be private.

Riding a mule provided only a reprieve from her exhaustion, which seemed to double nightly. But the swaying of the animal's stride was torture for her equilibrium. And so, she would walk as long as her legs would allow, then ride until she became sick. This was a repeating sequence of events until they finally reached the fields of wildflowers near Paradise on the afternoon of the fourth day.

Being the beginning of October, the flowers weren't nearly

as lovely as they'd been a few weeks earlier. A light dusting of snow covered the green fields, with muted colors peeking through.

It smelled of frosty evergreens, and she remembered her other climbs on this mountain—memories that already felt far away. The breeze caressed her face as she patted her mule's gritty neck. It huffed loudly in response.

They had been farther up the mountain when Peter had exposed the evil inside him. It turned her stomach to think of it.

Yet, here she was, back on the mountain. She may never know if he had meant to kill her or just scare her from ever returning. If his aim had been to make her afraid to climb again, he had not succeeded.

This fact gave her great pleasure, giving her a boost of energy, and she grinned.

When they finally reached the lake of reflections, it was the loveliest sight of all. It was the third time she'd seen her face shining back at her in the still waters. She could look up and see the mountain, crisp and clear, in both the sky and the calm lake. It was a paradise of its own—no wonder they had named the area as such.

As she stood admiring the view, Ben pulled something out of his pack.

"A new tradition. Belgian chocolate on the mountain, preferably in this beautiful spot."

Anna laughed. "I'll never say no to chocolate, especially your fancy European bars."

They each popped a chunk into their mouths, and Anna couldn't believe the richness. "This is the same kind you gave me when you were teaching me to shoot a bow, isn't it?"

"Indeed. It's called *Côte d'Or*. French for Gold Coast, where the cocoa beans come from in Africa."

"I thought it was Belgian chocolate?"

"Yes, the chocolate is made in Belgium, but the beans come from the golden coast of Africa—*Côte d'Or.*"

"Well, I couldn't love this new tradition any more."

It felt as if each year on the mountain was building on the one before, creating a beautifully layered experience, each one colored with what she had enjoyed or struggled with on each trip.

When they reached the camp, she was grateful for the rest but also ecstatic to begin talks with Fay about the club. There was something illicit about it, although it was perfectly legal. She knew it baffled some men and made others angry.

Fay's voice was strong and musical when she found them. "Welcome to the clouds, my friends."

"We're so happy to be here. Thank you again for inviting us," Anna said in the grass.

"I can't imagine anyone else I'd like to start the group with," Fay replied, fanning her skirts around her to sit next to Anna. "How was the trek here?"

"Well, I appear to be with child, so that has made things slightly more complicated, but I think we've done a fine job of making it."

"Congratulations are in order! Maybe one day I'll settle down as well."

"Of course, I don't plan to settle down really," Anna added quickly. "Just a few more months of being in this condition, and I'll be right back out in the woods and on the mountain."

Ben glanced at her sidelong, and she cringed inwardly at her choice of words.

"Absolutely. Can't hold this woman down, ain't that right, Mr. Chambers?" Fay said with a twinkle in her eye.

"Oh, I wouldn't even try," he replied. "I'm going to get our tent set up while you ladies catch up."

"I don't mind helping—"

"And I don't mind doing it so you can talk," he said with a grin.

As John and Ben found a flat area with still-hot embers in a makeshift fire hole, they got to work. Anna watched them with appreciation. Exhaustion had settled into her bones. Ben knew so, and she was grateful for his insistence that she remain with Fay.

"The truth is that I've been feeling ill," she said, glancing at Fay.

"I hear that's common."

"Is it?"

Fay shrugged. "I think so? I'm unsure. It should get better the further you are along. Are you alright to stay here tonight?"

"Absolutely. I wouldn't miss it. I've been thinking of nothing else since I got your letter."

"So, what are your thoughts on a mountaineering club for women?" Fay asked.

"I think it will make women feel more comfortable to be associated with the mountain and such outdoor activities."

Fay nodded. "Likewise. It's long overdue, if you ask me."

By the time they had set up camp, Anna's stomach was angry with hunger. It was a balancing act indeed to keep it happy these days.

For a meal, they dined on bread and cheese around the fire as the sun set.

"So, what first made you interested in climbing the mountain, Miss Fuller?" John asked.

"Yes, we've brought a reporter along, and he will ask many questions," Anna said as she took a bite of bread.

"Well, I don't mind at all. Actually, funny you mention that, because I quit my job as a teacher this summer. You're looking at the first female reporter for the *Tacoma Ledger*."

John's jaw dropped as he stared at Fay, and he was speechless for once.

Anna reached a hand to pat Fay's shoulder. "That's incredible. Congratulations are in order for you as well, I see!"

"Thank you. I can't wait to get started. Next week, in fact. My column is 'Mountain Murmurs.' I plan to interview those who have climbed our beloved mountain. I think I'm also supposed to cover some climbing-related social events." She shrugged and took a bite of cheese, then wiped her hands off on her skirts.

"I will look forward to reading your column, Miss Fuller," John said.

"Thank you. And I hope to meet many modern-day climbers such as I have in this fine company."

Ben leaned toward the fire to stoke it. "And so that's how you'll spread word about the alpine club. Will it be just for women?"

Anna exchanged glances with Fay.

"That had been the intention, yes," Fay said.

"Why purposely exclude the men?" John asked.

"Why, it's not a matter of leaving them out," Anna said. "Only to create a club that would ordinarily be only for men but which allows and even celebrates women climbers."

"I see," John said.

Twilight had come, and the purplish glow of the

surrounding snow was thick with promise. It was adventure waiting to happen—dreams and delight ready to be explored. Sitting by the warmth of the fire, Anna imagined plunging her bare feet into the whiteness. A thin, crisp layer of ice would cover the top, but it would give way to the powder underneath. Or perhaps it wouldn't give, for all snow is different. It might hold fast and sticky, and she would have to plunge her toes into its depths. A mystery she'd love to discover.

"I think it's a fantastic idea," Ben said. "And I look forward to reading your column as well, Miss Fuller. We make it down to Tacoma from time to time, and we'll be sure to pick up the paper and read your work."

Fay opened her mouth to speak and then hesitated. She cleared her throat and began again. "I suppose it wouldn't ruin the scheme to include men. It would certainly double or triple participation. And I do like the idea of having men and women on equal footing in regards to membership. What with us being so close to having the vote. If we can climb mountains, we can surely manage a vote!"

Anna nodded earnestly. "I would also be fine with including men, as long as we count the women's vote equally important in club matters."

"Well, we have time to decide all of this. For now, it's just the two of us." Fay looked up, and her eyebrows lifted in thought. "Or the four of us? What do you say, gentlemen?"

"Aye," said Ben, putting his arm around Anna's shoulders.

John grinned. "It would be an honor."

Ben passed the water canteen to Anna, but she waved it away. She couldn't imagine fitting one more drop into her stomach. The queasiness had returned, despite the joy of the moment.

The next morning boasted a glorious sunrise with clear

skies and dark blue edges. Anna felt heavy, a lesser version of the altitude sickness she had experienced previously at a higher elevation. Her mouth was dry, and her body movements seemed exaggerated in the effort it took. A slight vertigo disturbed her presence of mind, but overall, the beauty of the alpine meadows overshadowed the discomforts. She realized that, in her current state, she must be more susceptible to these minor bodily disturbances.

As she buttoned her shirt and pinned her mother's cameo at her collar, a wave of nausea gripped her. She hurried out of the tent and just barely made it to the edge of camp before she was sick in the grass.

She caught her breath and looked around. No one had seen, or if they had, they had pretended not to. After all, nausea was overwhelmingly common while climbing mountains of this elevation, but usually it was the climbers coming down from the heights that were ill.

She kicked some snow over the contents of her stomach and spun around to return to the tent. Ben was already bringing their bag out so they could carry it along to have lunch at the lake.

"Feel better?" he asked.

"Not really, but I'm fine. Certainly can't blame it on the lack of fresh air."

"I suppose not," he replied, putting the small pack onto his back, then offering his arm. "Shall we?"

She laughed and took it as if she was donning a gown and they were about to walk up a grand staircase. He made everything more fun, especially when he was silly.

After a quick breakfast, the four of them hiked back to the lake of reflections. On a day like this, with no hint of wind, there would be two mountains, one perfectly reflected in the glassy water. The hike was short, the weather agreeable, and the water was so pristine that it seemed almost unreal.

They found a spot near the water and put blankets down to sit on. Anna was thirsty but hesitant to drink too much or too quickly, fearing she'd make herself sick again.

The breath of the mountain pushed against her back, the crisp air a balm to the fire in her stomach. The deep blue sky was so far above them that it seemed as if it hung in the space beyond the atmosphere. Usually, being on the heights of the mountain made her feel as if she could touch the sky, but now she felt farther than ever from it.

"Are you sad to head back tomorrow morning?" Ben asked her.

"Quite so. I could live up here, with the cool breeze and impossibly fresh air."

"Perhaps we can come camp here again after the baby is born. Next summer."

She bit the inside of her cheek. How easy would it be to travel and camp with a little one? Especially a babe of only a few months.

And then she thought of the river crossing that was always treacherous. There was no reasonable purpose to make an infant cross it. Her heart sank.

"I would like that," she said. "But the river gets so high in the summer. Perhaps we can meet in Yelm, though." Then she turned toward Fay. "What do you say? Next summer?"

"You can count on it," she replied, crossing her legs at the ankles and reclining back on the weight of her arms.

She tried not to think of what she would miss out on because of having a baby. She was getting used to the idea of being a family of three. Adventures with a little one, being a mother, and all the beautiful things that came with it.

They stayed in the afternoon sun as long as they could before the chill pushed them back to camp where the fires burned hot. As she stood and the four of them started back to base camp, Anna's heart raced. A painful type of pounding, and she wasn't sure if it came from the disappointments layered just beneath the surface of her heart or if she might be sick again.

Despite the cool wind, heat radiated through her torso. A small mercy, she supposed.

The next morning, she awoke covered in sweat. She dressed and slipped outside the tent for fresh air. She breathed deeply of the mountain scent. It gave her life, and she didn't want to leave, but she was soon retching right next to the tent. Ben came out at once, and she turned her back to him to be sick again.

As soon as she straightened herself, she became so thirsty that the longing took over every other thought. "I need water."

Ben jumped back into the tent to grab the canteen and thrust it at her. "I wish you would have drunk more yesterday—"

She silenced him with a cool glare. "I didn't want to keep being sick! Every time I vomit, I lose much more water than the small sips I get down."

"I'm sorry." He lifted his hands in surrender. "I'm just trying to help."

"I'll pack the rest of my things and let's go home."

She didn't know what else to say. It was all she could do not to yell or scream or hit something. So many emotions flowed through her, and her heart was still pounding. The urge to suck every ounce of water from the canteen was overwhelming, but she could already feel the contents of her stomach swirling.

What an odd kind of torture.

Inside the tent, she blew out an exhausted breath. She had no energy to walk three days, despite her deep desire to do so. She'd have to ride the mule most of the day, which would make her even more sick. Perhaps Ben and John would be interested in staying one more day to let her rest and get her strength back. Maybe the trip there had taken more out of her than she knew.

As she adjusted her pants, which always seemed to inch up, she realized there was blood on them. At first, she thought she must have sat down on some berries or cut herself, but then the truth settled on her.

Her racing heartbeat returned, and so did the overwhelming thirst. She hadn't had nearly enough, and she knew it.

Had that caused her to bleed?

Her eyes teared up, but she angrily pushed them away. She had no fluid to waste.

There wasn't an enormous amount of blood, but the doctor had warned her that this might happen if she overdid it on the mountain.

Gathering herself, she took in the deepest breath she could manage, put her things together in their pack, and then walked outside where Ben still waited.

"Something's wrong," she whispered. "I'll ride a mule today, and let's hurry home—fast as we can."

"What happened?" he asked, concern etched in his brow.

"Some bleeding. Not a lot, but it shouldn't happen at all."

He stared, unmoving. Then, after a pause, he nodded and began to take the tent down. Anna took another sip of water, even though it turned her stomach in the most vicious way. She wanted to get back to the city. See the doctor—well, a different doctor. Speak to someone who knew about these kinds of things. And at the moment, she was as far away from those types of people as possible. Hopefully, there would be a doctor in Yelm.

They had already said their goodbyes to Fay the night before, so the three of them slipped away from camp without delay. They had told John only that Anna didn't feel well and wanted to hurry home.

As she mounted the mule, she closed her eyes and hoped that everything would be all right.

# CHAPTER ELEVEN
## THE KIND NURSE

*Elizabeth*

Elizabeth slipped out of her calico and decided she should wear a proper walking dress to meet Mr. Bailey. She had just returned from visiting with the secretary at Grace Hospital, and they were happy to take her on as a volunteer student nurse for a day. It had taken weeks to muster the courage to ask, especially after Dr. Glazier's ominous words. Perhaps it stemmed from the exhilaration of being asked on a walk by Mr. Bailey—a small confidence boost.

They would be expecting her the very next day, and just the thought made her head spin.

Why was it that life was either a gloomy spiral or maddeningly wonderful?

She took the dress from the bed where it lay. The dark blue bodice had braided sleeves, vest, and collar, and the seams that came from under the sleeves drew to a point at her waist. A slight puff in the shoulders accentuated the high collar with braided silk to match the arms.

Her skirts were a thick plaid of gray, white, and light blue of the tartan style.

She looked at her reflection in the mirror. Her fair hair was swept up into a fashionable bun, and the blue of her dress brought out her eyes, which made her feel pretty. Pretty didn't matter so much in a hospital, but it mattered a great deal when a man wanted to take a lady on a walk. She was expecting Mr. Bailey at any moment.

When the knock sounded on the door, her heart pounded.

Why exactly did he want to take her for a walk?

When his eyes met hers, she knew they had a connection. It was a mysterious thing, something she'd never had with anyone before, not even Levi.

When he'd been courting her, she had held him in high regard—she'd thought him good-looking and kind. But with this man, it was different.

She did not know what drew Mr. Bailey to her. But perhaps he had a few secrets of his own, and maybe he could tell a kindred spirit when he saw one.

"Good afternoon, Miss Grayson," he said with a slight bow. "Are you and your brother ready for a stroll?"

"We are. Where shall we go?" She fastened her hat in place, careful that the blue velvet and straw piece wouldn't budge.

"I was thinking the park would be nice. Unless there's somewhere else you'd rather go?"

She smiled as her brother came up behind her.

"Afternoon, Mr. Bailey. Lovely day, isn't it?"

"The park sounds perfect," Elizabeth answered with a graceful nod.

As soon as she said the word *perfect*, her mind fixated on it.

Nothing was ever truly perfect, was it? Neither beauty nor science. But that wasn't what she'd meant anyhow.

She couldn't help but wonder about her own motivations in this unexpected stroll. As a little girl, she'd always imagined falling in love with someone intelligent, like a doctor or a teacher. Not a born genius, but a man who worked hard to learn and expand his mind as she did.

But now, she had resigned herself to possibly never marry. To live with someone and spend every day together would force her to bare her soul. That person would see her checking things, obsessing over details that she knew she ought to ignore.

She'd grown accustomed to living with her parents and brother, of course. Her parents simply thought her odd and didn't pay that much attention to her either way. Also, she'd grown clever at hiding the ailments of her mind, for pure fear of ending up the exact way that the doctor had mentioned—in a hospital for the insane. And her brother seemed to understand the necessity of discretion.

"Well, I think you're going to have to tell me a little more about yourself," she said. It wouldn't do to be rude to the man, no matter what either of their true motivations were.

Would he offer his arm, or should she take her brother's?

"Of course." Mr. Bailey put his hat back on his head and turned toward the street.

Her brother offered his arm to her, and Elizabeth sighed. Probably for the best. Mr. Bailey came to walk on the other side of her as they started toward the park where the apple orchard was.

"Let's see. I live with my grandmother, who has raised me since I was about ten. She has difficulties with her hands these days, so I do most of the gardening and shopping for her."

*What odd tidbits to open with.*

Her heart was melting. How sweet was this man? "Then you must stay quite busy."

His lips curled up in a smile, and two dimples appeared in his cheeks. He really couldn't be any better looking.

It was too soon to ask what had happened to his parents. Were they dead?

"And we already know that you're an expert with your tomatoes," she added.

James laughed. "Mother will quite appreciate your help this spring. She loves tomatoes but hates taking them out of our own stock at the store."

"I'll be happy to share the knowledge that I do have about them. My grandmother has been perfecting her seeds for decades to flourish in the climate here."

Once they reached the park, James paused. "I have an idea I must write. Mr. Bailey, would you be so kind as to accompany my sister for a moment while I take a seat on the bench?"

"My pleasure," he said, tilting his head toward Elizabeth graciously. He offered his arm.

She took it, and even though part of her had been hoping to, dread suddenly filled her.

"I'd be happy to show you our garden someday. If you're interested," he said, searching her eyes.

Elizabeth's mind was reeling. A cold sweat had taken over her body, and she was grateful when he started walking and turned to look forward.

"If I'm interested?" she asked, trying to recall his question.

He glanced at her again, and she met his eyes, which were dancing.

"Interested in my garden, Miss Grayson. Unless there was something else you're interested in?"

She blushed. He was teasing her, but she wasn't as witty with her words or quick on her feet as he was.

"I'm sorry." He put his hand over her gloved hand that rested on his arm, and the warmth was electric. "I didn't mean to tease. Why don't you tell me a little about you now?"

She nodded and swallowed. "Well, I've finished high school, and I'm interested in becoming a nurse. Tomorrow, I'll be volunteering at Grace Hospital, actually."

"That's wonderful." He turned to look at her again, and their eyes locked. "That suits you."

"You think so?" she asked, finally warming up to the conversation.

"Indeed. Or rather, I believe so. I still don't know you all that well, do I? Tell me more."

She smiled and tried to think of the best thing to share. "I had quite high marks in school. I've always been interested in the sciences. They're so definite, you see. Something either works or it doesn't. There's little room for doubt."

It felt good to voice those thoughts. They had been in the back of her mind for years, but she hadn't quite found the words for the feeling. Doubt—it seemed to be her worst enemy and her constant companion.

He was quiet, and she immediately regretted opening up.

Had that been too much?

"So, you took your academics seriously."

"I did," she said, proud of herself but thinking that perhaps she shouldn't be. "Knowledge is the foundation of everything else in life. I hope to always be learning, through books and—"

Mr. Bailey smirked with amusement in his eyes, which stopped her words from flowing.

"Good for you. I can't say that I think much of school, but that's great that you have a natural aptitude for it." His tone was dismissive.

"Well, I had to study to get good marks. It certainly wasn't just something that happened easily."

Usually, she preferred for people to think that it came easily for her, but the way he put it—the way he was responding to what most people appreciated—was throwing her off. And it took little to stall her in conversation.

"I understand," he said quickly. "No offense, truly. I've just never put much stock in academics. Morals and good common sense seem more valuable. Practical experience, that type of thing."

Her stomach dropped when she realized he was in earnest. She didn't respond but looked into the horizon.

James returned and offered his arm to her, and she gladly let go of Mr. Bailey. It was getting more and more difficult to read him.

Her mind raced as her doubts worked their dark magic. And there were plenty of worries ripe for the picking.

THE NEXT MORNING, Elizabeth woke with a sense of dread, which wasn't all that unusual. She'd become accustomed to it —always there. Sometimes, she could ignore it well enough, and other times it sucked her into a spiral of thoughts that were hard to escape.

But today, she would be useful at the hospital, and no matter how her mind or body felt, this was a wonderful day.

It had to be.

It must.

When she checked into Grace Hospital, a tall man in a white lab coat came careening down the hall with a clipboard. He was thin, his graying hair disheveled. With a firmly set jaw, he gave her a puzzled look before his eyebrows raised.

"Volunteering?" he asked.

"Yes, sir. Thank you so much for having me."

"Thank you kindly for coming. I'm Doctor Roland." He nodded quickly, then kept walking.

Elizabeth hesitated a moment before glancing back at the lady behind the desk who made a shooing motion with her hands. She rushed to follow.

"Today, I'll give you a quick tour of this floor. If you decide to volunteer again in the future, you can participate."

She nodded somberly, then they were off again. Walking in and out of hallways, curtains being whisked to the side, the smell of alcohol and anesthetic surrounding them. It felt surreal, and yet she wasn't nervous, just energized.

One patient, a young girl, had split her lip, and Doctor Roland was deciding whether she needed stitches. Probably not, she guessed, but she kept quiet. She ought not to interact with patients, just watch like a ghost.

An old man who had fallen on his house steps was the next patient. The doctor manipulated the man's ribcage, gave him a tonic, then they were on to the next.

The morning whizzed by with barely a chance for Elizabeth to catch her breath. She loved how fast everything moved there. Usually, it was her mind moving so quickly, but she could see how the rapid pace of a hospital could be addicting and distract her from the otherwise bothersome thoughts she had grown accustomed to.

"Alright then," the doctor said without looking over at her. "We'll check on this next patient, and then you can take a break to eat your lunch."

She could smell the blood before they entered the room, and a metallic taste filled her mouth as if it hung in the air. A woman with a white face clutched her arm to her chest while two nurses tried to coax a blood-soaked towel away.

Elizabeth smiled seeing the nurses, knowing that might one day be her. She wondered what it would be like to wrestle with a patient who was in pain but who needed to be helped.

The doctor waved the nurses away and stepped forward.

"What happened?" he asked the woman in a smooth voice.

The woman simply shook her head, her teeth chattering. Elizabeth's hands tingled so she made a fist, then spread her fingers to keep them from going numb. Her heart pounded, and the smell of blood was bothering her more than it usually did. She remembered the dried blood on her fingers the day of the earthquake and the stain that had coated the walkway outside Grayson's Grocer.

Slowly and silently, the woman unwrapped the towel. Blood dripped down her elbow and trickled to the tile floor below.

Elizabeth's world tilted, and there came that itch she couldn't scratch somewhere in her mind. It ached and gnawed at her, filling her with terror.

Nausea whirled in her belly, and she thought she might throw up, but her feet froze to the tile. She could vividly remember the blood that dripped off the little boy's leg the day of the earthquake.

Looking down at her hands, she made sure there wasn't

any left on her fingers, which she knew was impossible, but doubt consumed her. She must see and touch her clean fingers to believe.

Taking a step back toward the door, she could already taste it. She didn't want to get any of this woman's blood on her.

Her arms went almost completely numb, and she turned to the nurses with a look of desperation—a cry for help. One of them looked disgusted with her and turned away.

The other one, the taller nurse who was far prettier, seemed concerned.

"Are you afraid of blood, dear?" Her lips turned down into a frown.

"I don't think so." She'd seen blood plenty of times, and it had never had this effect on her.

Doctor Roland continued caring for the patient with the help of the other nurse who had come to his side.

Elizabeth's chest ached with embarrassment.

The tall nurse quickly shuffled her away into a sitting room. "Can't have you swoonin' in front of the doctors, ya know?"

"I understand," Elizabeth said, averting her gaze. "I'm so sorry. This is humiliating."

"Are you sure you're alright?"

She nodded. Even if she knew how to explain what was going on in her mind, she wouldn't have told this woman or anyone else at the hospital.

Would they ever allow her to volunteer again?

"Well, my name is Meg. That other nurse is Eleanor. Do let us know if you need anything."

She left Elizabeth alone in the sitting room.

The world felt askew.

All her dreams of becoming a nurse were slipping out of her grasp.

Was she even capable?

A lady nearly fainting was certainly not out of the norm in polite society. But if anyone at the hospital realized there was a bit of madness in her, not to mention a newly manifesting and irrational fear of blood, her reputation and her future would be in serious jeopardy.

Nobody could find out. And she needed to act as normal as possible.

# CHAPTER TWELVE
## OLD-FASHIONED DOCTORS

Anna

When they stopped to rest for dinner and set up camp, Anna couldn't wait to check on the bleeding. She had managed not to be sick again that day and had taken small drinks of water whenever she could manage it.

Could it be that she was losing her baby?

She had only just started to get excited about it the day before. The timing felt cruel.

The horror and regret and impatience all mixed into one terrible mess.

When she could steal away to look, there was another small amount of blood. Enough to make her pulse quicken, but not so much as to lose all hope.

By the next morning, she and Ben were both worried terribly. He was unusually quiet that day, and they made such good time that they almost made it all the way to Yelm, but they decided to camp for one more night.

When they finally arrived in town early the next day, Ben went in search of a doctor. Anna waited with John for what seemed like hours, and just as they started snacking on the pears they'd found on a tree, he returned.

"A medical student on holiday from school. That's the best I could find."

She nodded and took the hand he offered to help her up from the log she'd been sitting on.

"It'll have to do."

When they arrived at the house, Ben knocked loudly. A young man answered the door—he was maybe twenty-five years old.

"Thank you for agreeing to see my wife, Mr. Atway."

"Of course. Happy to be of service. I'll do whatever I can."

He ushered them into the sitting room of his parents' home. After Anna had explained the pertinent details, the man nodded.

"How advanced is your condition?"

"I'm only in the second month or thereabouts," she said uncertainly. "We expect the baby at the end of April."

Mr. Atway brought out a leather satchel that reminded her of Dr. Evans'. She pushed the thought out of her head and focused on the tools he pulled out. One appeared to be a rubber hose with small devices at each end. The other was a wooden instrument that looked oddly like a trumpet.

"It might be too early to hear a heartbeat anyway, but I'll try. We might get lucky." He turned to Ben. "I'm sorry, but I'll need absolute silence if there's any hope of hearing a heartbeat at this early stage. Could you please step out of the room?"

"I'll be quiet as a church mouse," Ben said, holding tightly to Anna's hand.

Mr. Atway nodded kindly. "I know you want to be here for your wife, but even your breathing will distract. And before you tell me you can just hold your breath—"

"I understand," Ben said, his shoulders slumped. He turned to her. "I'll be just out the door if you need me."

She squeezed his hand. "I love you."

Ben's eyes became misty, and he only nodded and put his hand to his chest. Then he hurried out of the room.

"Let's see here," Mr. Atway said. "I have two options. This one is an older instrument, but it's tried and true. I'll try it first. Please recline in the seat and put your hands to the side so I can put the end of the device on your stomach. Let me know if I'm putting too much pressure on you."

She nodded.

"So, you've come back from the mountain, have you?"

"Yes, and we summited in early August," she said, watching carefully for his reaction.

"You don't say? Congratulations. I sure love clear days when I can see the mountain."

And that was all he said as he adjusted the tool in his hand. Anna sighed, relieved. She detected no judgment, and it put her at ease.

He put one end of the wooden instrument on the outside of her shirt and put his ear to the other end. She held her breath and attempted to be as still as possible.

After a few long minutes, he shook his head and reached for the tubular tool.

"Would it be better if I lifted my shirt? So you can put it directly on my skin?"

The man blushed and glanced toward the door where Ben stood. "Let me check with your husband."

He scurried out of the room, and she heard low whispers. Of course, Ben would say yes if that would give a better chance of hearing a heartbeat.

When he returned, his face was flushed pink, and he nodded. "Yes, please lift your shirt, and perhaps pull your . . . pants down a small bit."

Anna did as she was told. He bent down close with the metal end piece of the tube against the flesh of her belly, and the other he put squarely in his left ear. With one finger, he plugged his other ear and went perfectly still, his eyes closed.

The room was so quiet she could hear her own blood pumping through her ears, and she wondered just how difficult it would be to listen to two separate heartbeats, when he could probably also hear his own in the pure silence.

Once again, she held her breath and relaxed her body. The cold instrument against her belly felt unnatural.

After a few silent minutes, the doctor sighed.

"Could you hear it?" she asked breathlessly.

"Let me say this first, Mrs. Chambers. It's likely too early to hear anything anyway, but I wanted to try in case that reassurance was possible."

"So, you heard nothing."

Ben cracked the door and walked to her side. She squeezed his hand, her eyes filling with tears.

"I heard nothing, but the good news is, based on what you explained about the small amount of blood, you have not lost your baby. Now, if the bleeding becomes heavier in the coming days, that will be another thing."

"Are you sure?" Ben asked.

"I'm not sure of anything!" the man replied, somewhat amused. "But I do know that losing a baby at this stage of pregnancy is much more involved than a few spots of blood. You will *know* if you lose the baby. Most likely sooner than later."

Anna began to cry, even though this was mostly good news. She had wanted something certain—hope to cling to.

"Try not to worry," Mr. Atway said, his voice turning sympathetic. "It's not common to bleed during pregnancy, but there are many healthy babies that come from pregnancies where some bleeding was present. Take heart, if you can. Worrying certainly won't help. It will only make you miserable."

Anna nodded and wiped the tears from her face.

"One word of caution, though. In certain cases, the mother is better off resting for the duration. I don't suspect you'd be keen on that. You seem quite active." He paused, half of his mouth twisting into a thoughtful frown.

"I thought that was only necessary in the last weeks of confinement," Anna said, hopeful there could be another way.

He shook his head, and his eyes were apologetic. "Usually, yes. But your bleeding isn't—ideal. You will feel much more comfortable when it stops completely. And I think the best way to do that is to plan to spend some time at home. And if you must go places, take a carriage or a streetcar. Walk very little and rest as much as possible for the next week. If the bleeding stops fully, then you could resume moderate activity. Daily walks, perhaps. Does that sound alright?"

A warm flush of embarrassment came into her chest, and she closed her eyes before bringing herself to ask her ultimate question.

"Was this caused by the activity?"

*If I lose my baby, will it be my fault?*

*Because I chose to hike halfway up the mountain?*

"From what you told me earlier, it sounds like you didn't drink enough fluids. That happens easily while hiking, but add the vomiting, and it can happen quickly. When you're with child, your body needs all the nourishment it can get. If it doesn't, it will either revolt or send you a warning. I believe your bleeding is the warning. Take care of yourself now, all right?"

She nodded, swallowing the lump in her throat. The dehydration was nothing she could have prevented, despite her best efforts. Unless, of course, she had stayed home entirely. She sighed heavily.

Yes, it would be good to go home and rest for a few days—see if the bleeding would stop entirely.

But what if the bleeding returned anytime she was active?

It would be a death sentence—to stay indoors, to avoid walking in the forest, to melt away into the domestic sphere. How could she live like that? Surely, she wouldn't be able to continue working at the bookstore every day, which pained her more than she could put into words.

But what was the alternative?

Losing her child?

She shot Ben a desperate look, then turned to face Mr. Atway. "I understand. I'll rest."

"I know this won't be easy for you, Mrs. Chambers, and I'm sorry for it. But think of it as a small, temporary sacrifice. To give your baby his or her best chance."

"Of course. Yes, that makes sense. Thank you for your time and your wisdom, Mr. Atway. I'd rather hear this from you than . . . from a doctor I don't trust."

He shook Ben's hand and put his hat on. "Best of luck to you both."

"Thank you, Doctor," Ben said, putting a hand on his wife's shoulder.

"Not a doctor yet," the man said with a self-deprecating shrug. "In the spring, you can call me that. But, again, these are the newest instruments the university uses. There's simply no way to verify the heartbeat at this stage. Hopefully, your doctor in Seattle—"

"Would you visit us?" Anna asked suddenly. "My doctor is horrid. If there's good news to be had, I'd like it to be *you* who tells us."

"I'd be happy to make it worth your while," Ben said. "Where is your medical school? You're just visiting your family this weekend, is that correct?"

Mr. Atway scratched the back of his neck with a look that said he was considering their odd proposition. "Actually, I attend the University of Washington in Seattle. I suppose I could make a house call. You might be in better hands with a more experienced doctor, though."

"Nonsense. You have the right tools, and you're nearly a doctor. When would be the earliest we might hear a heartbeat?" Ben asked.

"If there's no more bleeding, that's your sign that everything is all right," Mr. Atway said, packing away his instruments back into his satchel. "But I suppose if you want the reassurance of the heartbeat, a little before halfway ought to get a clear sound. In the fourth or fifth month. Perhaps before. And you'll likely feel kicks around the same time."

"Great. Perhaps the end of November?" Ben asked, glancing at Anna for confirmation.

She nodded. "Yes, that sounds about right. Would that work for you?"

Mr. Atway let out a hesitant sigh. "Let's plan on it. Write down your address for me, please, and I'll send word when the time draws near."

Ben scribbled on a piece of paper while Anna wiped her face dry. There was hope. It felt weak and faint, but as he had advised, worrying would only make her miserable. Not that she could help it.

As they boarded the train to Seattle, she put a hand to her stomach. The tears kept coming silently, and she attempted to wipe them away before Ben saw them. He was insistent that she wasn't to blame, and that everything was fine—he just knew it. Nothing could dissuade his eternal optimism.

Now more than ever, she wanted this baby. The threat of losing it, or of that possibly still happening, had awoken something inside her—that maternal instinct. She had been afraid it would lie dormant completely until she held her son or daughter in her arms, but now here it was.

"The bleeding will stop as soon as we're home and get you situated," Ben said with a reassuring smile on his face.

"Yes, hopefully. Though I can't help but worry. I know I shouldn't, but what if it starts right back up again tomorrow? There's no certainty anymore."

"We'll take a carriage from the station, and I shall carry you into the house myself. Right onto your favorite chair that overlooks the mountain. You must stay there and read books while I bring you copious amounts of water and food."

She laughed. "Well, that sounds dreamy. I can't argue with any of that."

"And I've been thinking. After speaking with the doctor—"

"The almost doctor," she reminded him.

"I thought you liked him?"

"I think he's far better than any of the other doctors in this town. But we mustn't take everything he says as gold."

Ben sighed and put both of her hands in his. "I'd like to purchase a carriage and two horses."

"That seems rather extravagant. And unnecessary—"

"He said that you need to be mobile as little as possible. If we have our own carriage, you can go wherever you like— library association meetings, your grandfather's house, to Emily's or Heather's."

"Wouldn't we also need a driver? Or would you be quitting work to accompany me around town?" The words came out haughtier than she meant.

"Well, no, I suppose not all the time—"

"I'm sorry. Forgive me," she said in a hurry. "This is like a new world for me. It's almost as if I'm going to be held captive. How long will it have to be this way?" Tears sprang up in her eyes.

Ben wrapped his arms around her. "I think everything's going to be all right. We just need rest."

"But the pressure is all on me. *I* need to rest."

"And I'll be there with you as often as I can. I want to make this easier for you. Just tell me how I can."

She sighed, squeezing her eyes shut to stop the moisture from coming again. "I can take the street trolley to most places. And if it's a planned event, we can make advanced arrangements for a carriage. That will cost considerably less than taking care of a team of horses, right?"

"Absolutely." He grew quiet, looking into her eyes with admiration.

She had barely thought past the possibility of losing her child. What if she remained pregnant but had to stay stationary for months on end? It was bad enough to feel ill all the time, but it would be far worse to be stuck inside forever.

She put her forehead to the cool window of the train and watched the tall evergreen trees blur as they sped by.

Once at home, after Ben had situated her comfortably in a chair and with all the windows open to let in fresh air, he handed her a letter that had been delivered in their absence. A yellow ribbon adorned the crisp white envelope, which Anna unfastened and tucked into her pocket.

*Dear Anna,*

*Thank you so much for the kindness of your letter. I'm grateful that we can still be friends, even though your brother is no longer courting me. First, congratulations on your pregnancy. Nothing makes me more delighted than the promise of new life. At this point in my life, I've had much experience caring for women who are with child and also helping during their lying-in times. Do let me know right away if you need any help. Finally, one word of warning. You mentioned that you have been ill. Don't let any old-fashioned doctors tell you it's by any fault of your own. That's pure nonsense.*

*All my best wishes,*
*Elizabeth Grayson*

Warm emotion filled Anna. She had shed all her tears for the day, but her gratefulness for Elizabeth overcame her. How dare her old doctor say that she didn't want her baby? It simply wasn't true.

Now that she was home and not being jostled by mules and trains, her stomach felt more settled. By the open window, the pleasant-smelling wind whirled around her like she was atop the mountain, and it soothed her.

What would her life look like in the following months?

It was impossible to know just yet, but she planned to visit Elizabeth to talk more about what she knew about being with child. Or invite her to an evening out.

She was done listening to old men who meant to shame her.

# CHAPTER THIRTEEN
## THE THEATER

*Elizabeth | November 1891*

On Friday afternoon, Elizabeth stared into her closet in despair. Suddenly, she hated everything she owned.

Finally, she donned her stockings and petticoats. She chose a dress of rose-colored cashmere and black silk. The slender skirt opened in a slit on one side only to reveal more skirts. Embroidered roses decorated the hem.

The full bodice was made of black silk with drooping sleeves of cashmere until just below the elbows, where the soft fabric joined silk once more in a cuff with pearl buttons. A rose-colored cashmere sash gave just the right touch. It crossed at the waist to create a belt with fringes of pearl drops, similar to the pearls around the high neckline.

She had spent the last few weeks practicing her violin, doubting her abilities to become a nurse, and staying indoors during the unusually cold autumn. After the small scene she'd made, she had little desire to return to the hospital. And the thought of how she might respond to the sight of blood again terrified her.

When her monthly courses had come, it had nearly taken her breath away. More than ever before, she'd been uncomfortable and on edge until it was over. Hopefully, she wouldn't sustain any type of bleeding injury soon. The fresher and brighter red the blood, the more nauseated it seemed to make her.

But for now, her cycle was finished, and she wouldn't be back at the hospital anytime soon, so she breathed a sigh of relief.

After she combed her hair and pinned it high on her head, she placed pearl earrings in her ears.

Anna and Ben Chambers had invited her to see a play at the theater, and they had suggested her brother accompany her, as they had two extra tickets. But James had conveyed this piece of information to Mr. Bailey, who had insisted he take her himself.

She hadn't seen him since their evening stroll a few weeks prior, and the offer had surprised her.

When she entered the kitchen, James watched her from the table. "Bringing out the jasmine perfume already?"

"Oh, hush." She felt her cheeks warming and turned away from him as she popped a peppermint candy into her mouth.

"Only teasing," he said apologetically. "Well, I still haven't seen *A Midsummer Night's Dream*. You'll have to tell me how you like it."

She nodded, her nerves tingling at the thought of how much time she was about to spend with Mr. Bailey. First, in the carriage, then on his arm at the theater, then seated closely for the entire play. Just the anticipation was intoxicating. But she must keep her guard up.

When a light knock sounded on the door, James answered and shook hands with his friend. Elizabeth's father was still closing up shop at the grocer, and so her brother would see her off.

"Miss Grayson, I'm here to escort you to the theater." Mr. Bailey gave a slight bow, lifting his top hat gracefully.

"I'm looking forward to it." She made herself meet his gaze, even though her legs weakened.

She kissed her brother on the cheek and then took Mr. Bailey's arm. He walked her to the carriage, offering his hand as she entered. They would meet Anna and Ben at the theater.

Once inside, he sat back against the plush burgundy seat with a grin. "And now you're alone with me."

There was no stopping the blush that came to her face, and she shook her head, looking out the window, wishing she had something clever to say.

"Sorry. But when you're ruffled, I feel like I can see a little more into your soul—know you more, I guess."

Elizabeth's breath caught. She didn't want anyone to know her any more than they had to. But with him, she already felt like he wasn't trying to find fault in her. And at the same time, he didn't yet know what was in her mind or what her soul was made of.

"I'm glad to see you again," she said, pulling herself together. "It was awfully kind of you to offer to accompany me to the play. Have you been before?"

"To the theater? Yes. I quite enjoy plays. Though I have not seen *A Midsummer Night's Dream* before."

She smiled politely. "I've never seen an actual play at the theater. I imagine I'll like it very much."

"Well, if you like love stories and fairies in the forest, you ought to like this one."

Elizabeth had only read one play by Shakespeare, *Hamlet*, and she hadn't liked it much. But that one was a tragedy, and the play this evening would be a comedy.

By the time they arrived at the two-story brick theater, her nerves had only just settled.

Mr. Bailey stepped lightly out of the carriage and offered his hand to help her out. As they turned toward the entrance, she took his arm, resting her gloved palm on his forearm.

She wasn't sure of his intentions. He had offered to accompany her to the play, but he hadn't asked to court her. He clearly enjoyed her company and was interested in getting to know her, but there was still so much she didn't know about him.

Was he simply doing her brother a favor by taking her to the play, or did he want to spend more time with her?

And was he a man that spoke sweetly and played with a girl's emotions, or did he have honorable intentions if the time came and she actually fell in love with him?

It was impossible for her to say without getting to know him more. But either way, there was so much in her heart and mind that she never planned to share and avidly hoped no one would ever discover.

Alas, there would be plenty of time to worry about those things. For now, she was at a fancy play with a handsome man who, at the very least, enjoyed her company. Somehow, his presence made her more comfortable in awkward situations, despite his teasing, which was a true gift. And surely his witty nature would rub off on her.

"There you are!" Anna greeted them from the far end of

the foyer with a wave. She sat in a leather chair, Ben standing next to her.

They walked over to join the Chambers', and all the while Elizabeth was admiring Anna's gown. It appeared to be made of white lace over green silk and was trimmed with rosettes. The skirts were draped in such a way that the swell of her belly was hardly noticeable.

She offered her hand, and Ben bowed slightly, taking her hand in greeting. "What a pleasure to have you join us, Miss Grayson. Anna tells me you've been corresponding."

He turned to Mr. Bailey and offered his hand. "Sir, thank you for joining us. I'm Ben Chambers, and this is my wife, Anna."

"A pleasure to meet you both, Mr. and Mrs. Chambers," Mr. Bailey said, shaking Ben's hand heartily. "I was more than glad to accompany Miss Grayson to the theater this evening, and I thank you kindly for the invitation."

Anna glanced at Elizabeth with a meaningful expression, which made her blush, then she offered a place for Elizabeth on her seat and smiled warmly. "Thank you so much for the letter you sent me. Which was in reply to my own letter. Even so, I appreciated it."

Ben and Mr. Bailey began a conversation of their own, standing above them.

"Of course," Elizabeth replied. "When do you expect your child to arrive?"

Anna sighed deeply. "The end of April is my best guess at this point. I'm in the fourth month now. I've heard I'll be able to hear the heartbeat soon with one of those special instruments."

"Indeed," she said, grinning. "And has your baby kicked at all?"

With a frown, Anna shook her head. "Not yet. That's why hearing that heartbeat will give me such comfort."

"Are you sure you've felt nothing? I've heard that at first it feels like a butterfly is moving around lightly in your stomach. Not so much a giant kick on the first go."

Anna's mouth dropped open and she grabbed Elizabeth's arm. "I *have* experienced something like that! That's the baby moving?"

"Most likely, yes."

She released Elizabeth's arm and reached up to squeeze Ben's hand. "Did you hear that? I think I've felt the baby move!"

Ben's eyes lit up, and a grin grew on his face.

"You don't say? Then that baby is just fine, isn't it?" He put both of his hands around Anna's. "Do you suppose we still need to have the student doctor fellow come up and check for the heartbeat?"

"Yes, darling," Anna said without looking up at him. "But oh my, this has been such a wonderful evening already. I haven't left the house in weeks, and I don't think even a grand play could make it any better for me."

Elizabeth grinned, locking her gaze again with Mr. Bailey's. She loved that she had knowledge to share and that it was about something she enjoyed so much. He seemed impressed with her, and that made it even sweeter.

Ben handed Mr. Bailey their tickets. "Why don't you find the seats and get settled. We will be in shortly."

Elizabeth smiled at Anna, who grinned back. She took the arm that Mr. Bailey offered, and soon she was alone again with her escort.

The inside of the theater was draped in luxurious silks and velvet. Deep reds and golden yellows on the tapestries, and the lush blue curtain on the stage was closed, hiding what lay behind it.

They both sat in their assigned seats.

Mr. Bailey rubbed his hands together in front of him. "I believe we have about ten minutes before the play starts. Would you like to meet our neighbors?"

"I would not," Elizabeth said, smoothing her skirts. "Do I seem like a lady who likes to make small talk with people I hardly know?"

As soon as she had said the words, she wished she could take them back. He hadn't meant anything by asking, but she needed to show her hand on this one. He might as well know some true things about her. That way, if he desired to keep spending time with her, he could, and if not, even better.

He only laughed. "I admire your honesty. And no, you do not seem like one to chat idly. When you have something to say, I listen carefully."

She looked away, a shiver of pleasure going up her spine.

"Can I interest you in a conversation with yours truly?" he asked, his eyes lighting up as she turned to face him.

Even on the balcony, the seating was squished together. They were face to face, and she wondered if he could smell the mint on her breath.

"I would like that. I'd like to know more about you," she said, facing forward again, pretending to inspect the audience below.

She was working up the nerve to ask him what she'd been wondering since the last time they spoke.

"So, you've been with your grandmother since you were ten," she said, trying to sound nonchalant. "What happened to your parents?"

His eyebrows raised thoughtfully, and he folded his arms over his chest.

"I haven't had to tell this story for a while." He smiled wistfully. "My mother left us when I was a baby, so I don't know what became of her. My grandmother thinks she changed her name and moved back to England where she'd come from. I've thought about trying to find her, but it appears she doesn't want to be found. It wouldn't be challenging for her to find me if she had a mind to."

Elizabeth had assumed both his parents were dead, so this caught her off guard. "I'm sorry. What a difficult memory."

She hoped he would keep going without being prompted.

He sighed and unfolded his arms, leaning forward and resting his elbows on his knees.

"Then it was just my father and me. He was a lawyer, and he seemed to love the rush of the court. The more knowledgeable he became about the law, the more he felt a responsibility to uphold it and find justice for everything. He worked late, studied law books incessantly, and one morning, I discovered him on the floor in his office." He swallowed and turned to face her. "I guess he'd been up late researching something and must have gotten worked up. He was already gone when I found him."

Elizabeth turned to face him and blinked a few times. "I can't imagine finding my father dead. I'm terribly sorry."

She reached to touch his arm, but then pulled away.

He watched her hand retreating with a half-smile, one dimple showing. "So, I've lived with my father's mother, my grandmother, ever since."

She shook her head. "That's so much to carry."

"But I pass as an authentic gentleman, don't I?"

"It seems so."

He reached out a hand, putting it over hers, and her heart raced. He seemed to be a kind person, and he had her full attention.

After a few seconds, he pulled his hand away and put both hands clasped together in his lap. "I apologize. I'll behave —promise."

Just as he said the words, the electric lights above dimmed. Ben and Anna slipped into their seats with friendly waves.

Anna took the seat next to Elizabeth and whispered in her ear. "I've heard this is a good one."

Elizabeth nodded her head with a small smile, and they both grinned with anticipation.

When the curtains opened, wooden frames that looked like a Grecian court filled the stage, and the play began.

The voices rang clear and seemed to reach every corner of the great room. The spirit of the theater was electric, and Elizabeth enjoyed herself at once.

A few minutes later, she glanced over at Mr. Bailey, who sensed her gaze. He turned to look at her as well. He lifted his eyebrows as if to ask if she was enjoying herself, and she grinned in return.

His shoulder brushed up against hers in their cramped seating, and the touch was comforting. The attentive way he looked at her made her feel seen in such a satisfying way that it covered the melancholy of her nerves.

In the play, there was thwarted love and fairies in the forest. The costumes were magnificent, and Elizabeth imagined it must have taken weeks to sew the detailed dresses and fairy wings.

When the play ended and applause filled the hall, Anna praised her favorite parts. "It was divine, don't you think, Elizabeth?"

"I quite enjoyed it. Thank you so much for inviting us."

"Of course, I didn't want Levi and Emily's tickets to go to waste just because they were out of town." As soon as she finished the sentence, Anna looked as if she regretted her words.

"Oh," Elizabeth said, her cheeks burning.

"I suppose I didn't need to bring up that detail. My apologies," Anna said, her eyebrows raised as if she couldn't believe she'd said it. "All the same, it was a pleasure to meet you, Mr. Bailey. And, Elizabeth, I'm so glad we got to share the experience of our first play together."

Elizabeth smiled and nodded. "Indeed. I hope you continue to feel better."

Ben offered his hand to Anna, and she lifted herself off the chair gently, her skirts fluttering. Elizabeth could see the faint bump of her belly.

"Thank you," she replied. "You should come and visit me next week, and we can have a proper chat."

"That sounds lovely."

They said their goodbyes and parted ways.

Mr. Bailey helped her into a carriage. Night had fallen, and the stars were twinkling above them in the cloudless sky.

Elizabeth sat back in her seat across from him with a sense of relief and a luxurious sense of belonging. Mr. Bailey flashed a smile without a word and looked out the window.

The first thing out of his mouth once the carriage pulled out onto the street was, "So who's Levi? You seemed utterly uncomfortable when his name was mentioned."

She shook her head as if the name meant nothing and hoped that her face reflected it. "He's Anna's brother. He courted me last year. Mostly through letters, but I had some family dinners at his house." She reached for a stray thread on the bosom of her dress but decided not to pull it.

He was quiet and nodded twice. "Did you grow tired of him?"

Elizabeth bit the inside of her cheek, trying to think of the best way to explain the situation. "To be honest, I feared he thought me too . . . strange. Or perhaps I never opened up to him. But he said in his letter that he would court his sweetheart from when he was younger."

His jaw rippled slightly, as if he were grinding his teeth, but he remained silent for a moment.

"He ended your courtship with a letter?"

Elizabeth laughed. That was the most concerning part of her explanation? "A telegram, actually. But he sent a full explanation by letter."

"And why would the man think you strange?" he asked with a frown.

*The man.* As if he didn't even want to say Levi's name again.

"Sometimes my nerves get the better of me," she said, wrapping her shawl around her shoulders tightly as a chill came over her. "And I'm often quiet."

His frown deepened. "Were you ever alone with him?"

"In the same manner as we're alone at this very moment, Mr. Bailey?"

Finally, he smiled, but his lips were tight. She could see that he was jealous and needed a confirmation that they had never been intimate.

"He never so much as kissed me. We were rarely unaccompanied—much of the time we were courting, I was with my aunt in Oregon."

His face relaxed. "Well, I'd like to kiss you right now."

Elizabeth shook her head at his brashness.

"Who says that?" she asked playfully, but her shoulders trembled all the same.

He laughed easily. "What? I can't say what's on my mind? Kissing you is on my mind."

Her mouth dropped open in a disbelieving smile. She snapped it closed and folded her arms over her chest, not knowing what else to say.

"Again, I'm sorry." He reached for her hand with a soft touch. "I never want you to feel uncomfortable. I just mean to be honest. And I hope you'll do the same."

She wanted to kiss him too, but she wouldn't say the words out loud. She wanted to tell him there was a perfectly good reason she hadn't opened up to Levi. And that he should expect the same.

"Elizabeth," he said, his voice quieter. "May I court you? I've already spoken with your father and brother. But I wanted to know your sentiments first. And give you a chance to warm up to me before you declined."

She froze. It wasn't unexpected, but how does one politely say this will never work in the end? That he should put his efforts into someone more willing to share herself.

But she enjoyed spending time with him. Even her fits of doubting seemed to improve in the days after seeing him.

He pursed his lips together in a straight line, which made his dimples show.

Before she knew what she was doing, she nodded. "I accept."

A grin spread across his face. "That's excellent news, Miss Grayson. I promise never to think you strange or fall in love with a former childhood acquaintance."

His response surprised her, and she delighted in the way he

looked at her. It couldn't hurt to spend a bit more time with him. If she had declined the courtship, this would probably be the last time she saw him.

He was still leaning across the carriage, holding her hand. Finally, he let go and settled back into his seat.

"I'll walk you inside," he said when they arrived, opening the door and jumping out at once.

As he helped her from the carriage, Elizabeth felt truly glad but, at the same time, she doubted her decision. This courtship very well may end up like it did with Levi.

If she truly planned never to get too close to anyone, then all she would ever have would be these moments of connection with men she might have loved if she'd been a whole person— a person who could handle life.

Likely, she wouldn't spend the rest of her life on Mr. Bailey's arm, but she planned to appreciate the time she got— to savor it and store it up in her heart for the lonely years she knew were ahead.

# CHAPTER FOURTEEN

## HOPE

*Anna | December 1891 | The Fifth Month*

For the library association meeting, Anna's grandfather had offered to gather a carriage and pick her up on the way so they could go together.

"I sure miss you at the bookstore, lassie," he said, kissing her cheek as she stepped into the carriage with as little movement as possible.

"I miss it too, Grandfather. It's been hard adjusting to this new reality, but my health has been good, and I'm grateful for that." She put a hand on her stomach, as had become her habit now whenever she thought of her child.

"I'm grateful for that too," he said, eyes shining. "You should speak with Adelaide before the meeting today. She and Emily seem to have become fast friends. Adelaide has a whole horde of children, and maybe she's had an experience similar to yours. I don't know, perhaps some advice to offer."

He pulled out a handkerchief to cough in, then folded it up neatly to put in the pocket of his trousers. His eyes seemed tired, but she knew he loved these meetings. She put her hand over his and squeezed.

Now that she had drastically cut back on outings and walking, the bleeding had not returned. But a sense of foreboding still followed her like a dark shadow. She tried to focus on what her little son or daughter's face might look like instead of the despair she felt about the bleeding returning, and a winter and most of spring inside the walls of her home.

Soon, the brick buildings of the city came into view. The crisp winter air was a pleasure, and she wrapped her white fur cape closer around her neck for the comfort of the softness. Frost still lined the grass at the bottom of trees where the sun hadn't warmed it.

When they arrived at the library, she found Adelaide, who was already speaking with Emily and pouring coffee. The refreshment table was covered with pumpkin pies and cranberry muffins.

"It's so good to see you, Anna," Emily said, giving her a gentle squeeze.

"Indeed, we're honored you could attend," Adelaide said, placing a cookie on her saucer. She glanced down at Anna's growing abdomen. "Congratulations again on expecting your first child."

"Thank you," Anna said, reaching for a slice of pie. "I thought perhaps you might have some wisdom to share about being a mother. Have you ever had to extend your confinement period?"

Adelaide shook her head. "No, but let me tell you, as

difficult as it can be expecting a child, it's much more complicated and challenging once they are in this world, God willing."

Emily glanced at her with her eyebrows raised.

Anna nodded and put a forkful of pie into her mouth. The cinnamon and nutmeg were in perfect harmony.

"I don't mean to make it sound like a troublesome time, but once children fill your house, there won't be much time for anything else."

"How many children do you have?" Anna asked, afraid of the answer.

"Right now, five."

Her stomach dropped, and she swallowed to prevent her face from reacting.

"On some days, it seems I can barely do anything but keep them fed and alive, let alone invite a friend over for tea. Even when the older children are at school, there are always a few small ones at home who need me even more than their older siblings." She turned to Emily. "That's why I still haven't been able to invite you over for tea like we've been planning."

Emily smiled widely. "I certainly wouldn't mind the children running around while we took our tea."

"Well, why haven't you said so!" Adelaide laughed loudly, throwing her head back joyfully.

An older gentleman, Charles Wesley Smith, called the meeting to order, and everyone took their seats. They began to discuss the association's tight budget. They received ten percent of the city's licenses and fines, but that didn't seem to add up to much.

Anna's mind began to wander. Adelaide's life scared her. It would be tiresome to have small children constantly needing things. How would she ever get outside to enjoy hikes in the forest with so many lives to look out for?

And not being able to visit friends because of mothering—it was too much, and it wasn't what she wanted.

⚜

ANNA HAD ARRANGED for Mr. Atway to come to their house to attempt to hear the heartbeat again. After Elizabeth had told her that the fluttering sensations in her belly were likely the movement of her child, she couldn't stop thinking about it.

The feeling of what might be little kicks and punches gave her hope. And since the bleeding had never returned, it was possible she was carrying a healthy child and that she could resume her normal activities.

When Mr. Atway arrived at the designated time, her heart thumped in her chest.

What if he still couldn't hear anything?

"Good afternoon, Mr. and Mrs. Chambers," he said jovially. "It's good to see you both again. Thank you for inviting me to your home."

Ben shook his hand and invited him into their living room. "Thank you for coming. We greatly appreciate it."

"Yes, thank you," Anna said. "I'm sure you must be nearly ready for a Christmas holiday with your family in Yelm soon?"

He nodded. "Yes, a small break from the university, and I'll get to eat my mother's fine cooking for a few days. Then I'm off for a residency in Oregon for the spring."

She smiled. "If you're looking for any fine women in the area, I know an eligible lady."

"Isn't Mr. Bailey courting her?" Ben asked with a look of alarm.

"Oh, I wasn't sure if it was serious. Are they courting? It wasn't obvious."

Ben shook his head and grinned. "Anyhow, I'm sure Mr. Atway is perfectly capable of finding women on his own."

With a laugh, Mr. Atway opened his satchel. "I mean, I certainly don't mind suggestions."

"Then we'll keep you in mind," she said, distracted now by the instruments he was pulling out of his bag. "You're pretty sure you'll be able to hear the heartbeat at this stage, right?"

"I do believe so, Mrs. Chambers. I hope so. How have you been feeling?"

"I lost my breakfast this morning, which has become somewhat of a ritual. But the bleeding never came back after I spent some time resting," she said, leaning back in her chair. "Though I still worry that it will."

Mr. Atway frowned. "Does the vomiting happen on any certain days more than others? Have you noticed a pattern of any kind?"

Ben stroked the whiskers on his face. "You mentioned that your nausea got worse after our short walk to the market last weekend, and then got better over the next few days when you stayed home."

Anna swallowed. There seemed to be a correlation between her movement and physical exertion and whether she could keep food down. She hadn't wanted to mention it, but it was the truth.

"Yes, I think the more I exert myself, the worse it gets, it seems," she said reluctantly.

"We just want you to feel as well as possible. Let's see what we can hear inside, shall we?" Mr. Atway sat next to Anna and looked toward Ben. "I'll tell you what. You can stay in the room unless I can't hear anything, and then I'll try again with you farther away."

Ben nodded and went as motionless as possible from across the room, his arms folded across his wide chest. His eyes were soft as he locked his gaze with Anna, which filled her with confidence and comradery.

She lifted her shirt to show off a small but swelling belly.

"I'm glad to see good growth since I've seen you last," Mr. Atway said, positioning his cool metal instrument against her skin.

There was a moment of silence that stretched too far, but then Mr. Atway's eyebrows shot up and he grinned. "That's a strong heartbeat I hear!"

Tears sprang to her eyes. The joy that she felt in that moment was something she'd never experienced before—better than being in light of the summit or even at the highest peak of the mountain.

Ben rushed toward her, his face full of excitement.

"I knew it! But I'm also relieved." A nervous laugh escaped from his lips.

"Would you both like to hear it?" Mr. Atway asked, taking the instrument away from his ear.

They both nodded and took turns listening to the faint thumping of their son's or daughter's heartbeat—the sound of life.

After packing his instruments back up into his satchel, Mr. Atway turned to Anna. "This is excellent news, of course. And the choice is yours regarding how much you need to restrict your activity."

Ben and Anna exchanged hopeful glances.

# CHAPTER FIFTEEN
## A CHRISTMAS POEM

*Anna*

On the morning of Christmas Eve, Anna woke in a festive mood. She rolled over, as much as her growing belly would allow, and peered over at her husband. He was still snoring softly, so she rose and dressed in the chilly light of dawn.

There was not yet any snow on the ground, which was disappointing but no matter. They would fill the day with baking and music and family. The growing Gallagher clan would boast six people, a dog, a cat, and a baby by springtime.

She admired their own evergreen tree that Ben had chopped down and that they had adorned with strings of popcorn and cranberries. Even though it was a tradition she'd always enjoyed around yuletide, it now reminded her of their wedding. The bells, and firepits, and eggnog—it had been such a beautifully festive way to become man and wife. She would cherish the memory always.

They would not light the candles on their tree today but save them for Christmas morning. Tonight, they would light the candles at the Gallagher home and watch them twinkle into the night until the wax became so low that it would be safer to blow them out.

Below the tree, a few small wrapped presents rested snugly, nearly hidden among the thick evergreen boughs. She inhaled sharply, enjoying the crisp smell that reminded her of being outdoors.

"Merry Christmas Eve," Ben said in a deep voice from the stairs.

She turned to greet with him with a grin. "And to you. I can't wait to see what you have wrapped up down here."

"I'm eager for you to receive them," he said, taking her into his arms. "Open this one right now. It's something I wrote for our baby."

He reached under the tree and pulled out a crisp envelope with a wax seal.

"That's my mountain seal," Anna said with a smile.

"Do you mind? I thought you'd like that little touch."

"I love it." She took the letter in her hands and broke the seal with care. "Would you read it to me?"

He nodded graciously as she handed him the folded paper. "This is what I imagine it will be like—showing the beautiful world to our son or daughter. We'll take him camping and hiking and climbing the mountain one day. We'll get to see the forest through his eyes. Can you remember the first time you went camping? Anyway, here it is."

## The Stars Out Here Are Free

The forest croaks and chirps a song
in shades of green and brown.
The ferns and moss will hum along—
while pinecones tumble down.

We'll pitch our tents among the frogs
to celebrate the sound
and then we'll flip the biggest logs
to scatter bugs around.

The trees are taller than the sky,
their roots snake through the trail.
We'll leap and jump them, soaring high,
and barely miss their tails.

To make a fire, sticks are found
and piled fat to thinner.
Around the flames, right on the ground,
we'll sit and roast our dinner.

At night, you'll hear the rain in slaps,
pajamas will get damp.
You'll dream of finding treasure maps
and sailing through the camp.

The night is darker than the sea
without a candle's light.
But all the stars out here are free
to sparkle through the night.

ANNA TOOK the page back into her hands with wonder. Behind the words, he had drawn stars twinkling in the sky.

"Oh Ben, it's beautiful!"

He shrugged, his cheeks turning slightly pink. "We have so many adventures yet to come. The three of us—we're going to have more fun than ever. I know how hard it was on you, only leaving the house in carriages for library association meetings, not hiking outside and in nature where you love to be. But now that we've heard that heartbeat, and you haven't had any more bleeding, I think you should resume all your normal activities so you can feel like yourself."

It had felt like an impossible choice, to deny her soul the things that made her feel alive—waiting, hoping that her baby would be born healthy. All the while, the wild gardens of the mountain and the deep coolness of the forest had been just out of reach. But now she knew it had been worth it, and she would have done it the whole nine months if she'd needed to.

"That sounds wonderful," she said, grinning.

She still had peaks to climb—Mount Rainier wasn't the only mountain in Washington. The silence, the crisp dark blue edges visible on clear days. The very heights suspended above.

"Everything's going to be all right, I promise," Ben whispered, squeezing her shoulders and holding her close.

Anna nodded and held him tightly. "Thank you. And such a lovely poem."

"I'm going to secure a carriage for the way there and back from your grandfather's house today, but only because I think snow is coming. Take your time getting ready, and we'll leave whenever you like."

AT THE GALLAGHERS', the festivities had already begun when their carriage pulled up. The smell of chocolate and peppermint greeted Anna's nose as she stepped into her childhood home.

"Merry Christmas, dear," Greta sang out, embracing her. "Shall we make some chocolate crinkles? How are you?"

"Pretty good," she replied. "We heard the baby's heartbeat!"

"Wonderful!" Greta put her hands to her cheeks in delight. "And you haven't had any more bleeding, right?"

"That's right. From now on I'm going to be able to do as I please, even if it does make my nausea worse sometimes."

Greta laughed. "I'm so glad."

Anna wrapped her arm around the older woman's waist. "Everything looks lovely here, and the tree is divine."

She admired the evergreen decked with candles and other small decorations she recognized from years past. Eyeing an extra apron on a hook, she reached for it.

"Let's get started," she said, linking arms with Greta and nearly dragging her toward the kitchen.

"You don't have to persuade me, dear!"

In the kitchen, the festive smells grew stronger. An apple pie baked in the oven, nearly finished, and all the ingredients for chocolate crinkles sat on the worktable.

They got to work right away, melting the chocolate, mixing the ingredients, and rolling the dough into balls. Finally, they covered them with powdered sugar until they looked like little snowballs.

While the cookies baked, they joined Ben and her grandfather in the living room just as Levi and Emily arrived.

They exchanged holiday greetings all over again before they settled into chairs in front of the fire, near the Christmas tree. Her grandfather lit the candles while Greta dashed back to the kitchen to remove the cookies from the oven.

She returned shortly with a tray of hot chocolate and cookies.

Anna smiled as her grandfather pulled his harmonica out of his jacket pocket and played "Silent Night."

When the song was over, Ben reached for her hand and smiled softly.

"How have things been going with the library association?" Levi asked.

"Great," Anna replied, smiling at her grandfather and Emily.

"I've sure enjoyed having these two fine ladies there for the meetings," her grandfather said. "They are making their acquaintances with other fine ladies and helping to support the Seattle Library."

Anna reflected on her work with the library. It was good to keep her mind busy with these types of things, but it was ultimately such ladylike work. Emily enjoyed it, but the only part that thrilled Anna was that Seattle had a working library that allowed town residents to borrow books they might not otherwise have been able to afford. The social aspects, and the ability to meet certain members of society, were not so tempting for her.

But she had needed to keep her baby safe and her mind active, and so it had been the right thing to be spending her time on. But now she was doing better.

"Yes, I've grown quite fond of Adelaide," Emily chimed in.

Anna remembered Adelaide's words about being a mother, and it left her cold. She tried to remind herself that it was only her experience and that the woman had an awful lot of children. She and Ben would only have the one, at least for a while, she imagined. All the same, she preferred to change the subject.

"I've been corresponding with Fay about the alpine club. There's to be another meeting over the summer, and we're hoping to go."

Ben put his arm on her shoulder and nodded. "Provided that Anna and the baby are both healthy enough for the trip."

"I'm sure we will be."

It helped to say the words out loud. That way they seemed more real, more likely to become true.

As night fell, the candles on the tree seemed to grow brighter, twinkling in the darkened living room. Her grandfather played the harmonica softly, and the conversation dwindled down to murmurs between couples. He didn't quite have the power in his lungs to play all evening like he used to, and so they all admired the shining tree in comfortable silence after he put the harmonica away.

In the candlelight, Ben broke the silence. "What day should we leave for the hunting trip, gentlemen?"

"I'd like to be home by New Year's Day—to spend with my wife," Levi said, kissing Emily on the cheek.

Suddenly Anna's heart pounded with hope. "Let me join you this year. *Please.* My health has improved, and I've been aching to be outside enjoying the fresh air."

Her grandfather lifted his hands in front of him as if to say he would not be the one to make that decision.

Levi scoffed. "Anna, no. More so now than ever."

She looked over to Ben in the dim light and it was difficult to read his expression.

"Are you sure that's safe, dear?" Greta asked in a thoughtful tone. "I know you're quite skillful at archery, but don't you think the dead animals and their innards might upset your stomach?"

She hadn't thought of that, but her spirit wasn't hindered.

Ben pulled her hand into his. "Let's think on this. I imagine it would be best to ease into that kind of activity. But tonight we should enjoy the holiday."

It was an odd thing for him to say. And it was strange for him not to jump immediately onto her side. He hadn't exactly told her no, but it wasn't the response she'd hoped for, especially from him.

"That's wise," Levi said, sinking back into his chair. "And I'm sure that after we've all thought about it, the proper and safe choice will emerge."

Anna glared at him in the candlelight.

After they had left for the evening, riding in a carriage with bells jingling, Anna couldn't stop thinking about how enjoyable a hunting trip would be.

"I'm doing quite well. I think the best thing for me is to do things I love while I still can."

"What does that mean?" Ben asked. "Having a child isn't going to change everything about your life. It's not as if you'll never be able to hike or be outdoors ever again."

"How do you know this?"

"Anna, you're worrying too much."

"What if we end up with five children and I have to spend the next decade tending them?"

Ben looked out the window and squinted his eyes. "I thought you wanted to be a mother."

Anna felt as if she'd been struck. "I do. I mean, I haven't a choice about it now, do I? But I would really like to join this hunting trip, and I know you can convince the others."

"I don't know, Anna. I feel especially protective of you

while you're carrying our child. I can't explain it. But I'm just not comfortable with it. What if you start bleeding again? Or accidentally get shot?"

"That's the same risk for anyone hunting."

Ben sighed, exasperated. "I'm sorry, but I have to say no. Please understand."

She was shocked into silence.

This wasn't like him—and it was offensive.

When they arrived home, Ben offered his hand for her to get out of the carriage. She took it without looking at him. She couldn't.

There was a sense of desperation in her bones—something telling her that she must act, now or never. And it was then that she decided she would go hunting with or without her husband's approval.

# CHAPTER SIXTEEN
## A SECRET OF HIS OWN

*Elizabeth*

Elizabeth hurried to dress and finish her various habits of checking things before Mr. Bailey was to arrive for dinner with her family. It would be the first evening they'd spend together since Christmas.

He had devoted Christmas Eve and morning to his grandmother but had come for a quick visit for tea in the afternoon on Christmas Day. As a gift, he'd given her a mink shawl, which she adored. It was just like him to give her a present that would make her more comfortable.

For him, she had embroidered a small replica of the whale painting that they had bonded over.

As she checked her candle again to make sure the wax was cooling, she realized that the urge wasn't as strong as it usually was. She wondered if her obsessions had loosened their hold, but she knew better. Surely not. It must be a temporary reprieve because of the exhilarating experience of falling for Mr. Bailey.

Hopefully, her family wouldn't make things even more awkward than they needed to be, as they often did, especially her mother. She had actually grown to feel quite comfortable in Mr. Bailey's presence. He didn't seem concerned about her reticence, and he wasn't uncomfortable when she fell quiet for a spell.

Just as she finished her afternoon tea, she heard a knock at the door.

Elizabeth rushed to answer it, but her father had already arrived and invited Mr. Bailey inside.

"Great to have you back, son," her father said, shaking his hand.

"Thank you, sir," he replied, taking off his suit coat and hat, then hanging them on a hook near the door.

"Have I mentioned how delighted I am that my daughter accepted the courtship?"

Elizabeth recalled how forward her father had been with Levi about suggesting upcoming wedding bells, and she'd been actively trying to prevent that.

"Just the beginning stages, Father," she said with as much of a casual air as she could muster. "Nothing too serious at the moment."

"Well, I just hope you both get to know each other and have fun doing it, while staying proper, of course," he said matter-of-factly, giving Mr. Bailey his best solemn face.

She'd never seen Mr. Bailey's eyes so wide. Her own embarrassment washed over her, and she shuddered at the awkwardness.

At that moment, her mother walked in from the kitchen,

face glowing with delight. "Mr. Bailey, what a pleasure. It's so nice to see you again. Do come in and make yourself comfortable. Can I get you some tea before dinner?"

"No, thank you, ma'am."

Her mother looked at Mr. Bailey with a smile that could only be described as eager. "Very well. Dinner will be served in a few minutes. Why don't you make yourselves at home in the sitting room?"

Mr. Bailey put his arm out for Elizabeth, apparently to walk the short distance to the sitting room. "I'm happy to spend time with Miss Grayson whenever she'll let me."

Her mother's eyes got wide, then crinkled as she grinned. "You're so kind. I'm glad she's finally enjoying the company of a *true* gentleman."

She glanced at Elizabeth with a meaningful look on her face.

Elizabeth gave her the slightest shake of her head and closed her eyes briefly in annoyance. Her mother responded by mouthing *I'm sorry* before spinning around and hurrying back to the kitchen.

Her father walked with them until suddenly realizing he had something to do upstairs, and so he left them alone to have a private conversation before dinner.

"Do you like pork, Mr. Bailey?" she asked, settling herself on a plump chair across from where he sat. "Because my mother is hoping dearly that you do. With a light mint jelly. We grow the mint in our garden over the summer months and dry the extra to have through the winter."

"I'm sure I'll like it very much. It's always good to have mint on the breath, don't you think?" He winked at her.

Her mouth opened slightly, and she shook her head. She

wondered if he remembered the scent on her breath when their faces had been so close at the theater.

"As if there was any possibility . . ." Her voice dropped to a whisper, and she glanced at the entry of the room. "As if we were going to be close enough to kiss tonight. Shame on you."

She laughed but could feel her cheeks blush.

"But it's nothing too serious at the moment, right?" he said meaningfully.

She tilted her head to the side with a mock pout. "You caught that?"

"It's perfectly fine," he replied. "I enjoy getting to know you in an unhurried manner."

There were butterflies panicking in her stomach as she smoothed her skirts over her legs. She couldn't think of how to change the subject.

"May I call you Elizabeth?"

She nodded. "And shall I call you North?"

"If you like. I've never particularly liked my name, but if it suits you."

"I think it's a wonderful name." She smiled kindly and then looked down at her hands.

"Have you been back to the hospital?"

Elizabeth sighed deeply. "No."

She had never told him what had happened. She had told no one.

"And do you still plan to pursue nursing?"

The conversation was going in a direction she wasn't comfortable with. She gritted her teeth as nonchalantly as she could.

He cleared his throat during her silence. "Let me ask a different question. What first made you interested in becoming a nurse?"

"When I learned of Florence Nightingale, it inspired me to help in the same way that she did, and still does, I believe."

"Tell me about this heroine of yours." North leaned toward her, putting his elbows on his knees.

"She's a nurse from England, and she took care of many soldiers during the Crimean War. And she championed the idea of structure and sanitation in the care of patients. She also established the Nightingale Training School for Nurses in 1860."

"That's fascinating," he replied. "But you don't plan to go back to the hospital?"

She frowned. How could she tell him she'd made a fool of herself and that she'd been too ashamed to return?

"No, but neighbors have come to me for help now and then." She looked down at her hands, then went on. "Just last week I help set a broken arm."

She wanted to add that, thankfully, there had been no blood, but she thought better of it.

"Excellent," he replied, leaning toward her. "I'm sure the hospital would be glad to have you anytime you wished to return."

"Dinner's ready," her mother called from the entryway. She smiled at the two of them in a way that embarrassed Elizabeth all over again.

"Shall we?" North offered his arm once more, as if intent to walk her from each room to the next.

With a small laugh, she took his arm. It seemed that she was the center of his universe, the whole of his attention focused on her. She didn't mind one bit being escorted through her own house on his arm.

Her mother had set the table as if for a royal guest. Mashed potatoes in a china bowl, thick pork chops, and little bowls of mint jelly at each place setting with miniature spoons.

"This looks marvelous, Mrs. Grayson," North said with gusto. "What a family dinner you've prepared. I'm truly honored."

With a blush, Elizabeth's mother waved her hand dismissively as if it were nothing. "Please, take your seats. Mr. Bailey, I've seated you right next to Elizabeth, of course."

North pulled out the chair for her, and she nodded with a smile as she lowered herself into it. He pushed the chair in behind her as she sat, then he took his place beside her.

"I'll plant some tomato seedlings on my windowsill in about six weeks, Mrs. Grayson. When they're ready, I'll bring them over to you. And some seeds as well, so you can plant some yourself."

She clapped her hands in delight. "I can't wait to get my hands on them. I'll have the best tomato garden around, save for yours, of course."

North grinned. "My pleasure, ma'am."

"Your grandmother must be so proud of you. A successful train conductor and a real green thumb."

His cheeks turned pink, something Elizabeth hadn't seen before on him.

"I certainly hope so. She might have preferred that I become a professor or maybe a philosopher. I never quite got into books the way she'd hoped."

"Perhaps you just haven't found the right book yet," Elizabeth said. "Have you tried reading any biographies of train conductors? Or magazines about gardening?"

"Those are good ideas," he replied, wiping his hands on his napkin. "I just don't think reading is all that important, but maybe you're right."

Elizabeth thought about that for a moment. She enjoyed the occasional novel, and she certainly enjoyed reading books and journals that expanded her medical knowledge. It wasn't even always for pleasure. Sometimes, it was just necessary.

That's probably what he meant.

"When I finished school, I didn't want to read for a while," she said. "But then I realized the value in continuing to learn new things as an adult."

"Elizabeth did well in school," her father said, "and we've always been proud of that."

At that, her chest warmed with the joy of being recognized. Lately, those moments had become rarer, and so she let herself enjoy when it happened. Although she'd had to spend hours and hours to get those good marks at school. It didn't prove her intelligence, but rather her ability to do her best and keep secrets.

"Thank you, Father," she replied, trying not to sound too pleased.

"How do you like the pork, Mr. Bailey?" her mother asked, suspense in the creases of her eyes.

North had grown quiet and seemed to be focused on his plate. "Quite delicious, as I knew it would be. What a fine cook you are."

Elizabeth glanced sideways at him and wondered if she'd said something that upset him.

After the meal, she excused herself and hurried to her room upstairs to find a book to let North borrow. A story about Florence Nightingale would be perfect, since she'd just told him about her, and he seemed interested to know more. Something short—perhaps that would make him read it quickly and not dislike the experience.

She found just the right one and joined her family as they were wishing North goodbye.

"You're always welcome over here for dinner," her father was saying, patting him on the back.

"Absolutely," her mother agreed. "Anytime. We sure enjoyed having you."

They both retreated to the living room to give the couple some space to say their farewells. But not too much space, as her mother lingered in the dining room, cleaning up after the meal.

Breathless, Elizabeth pushed the book into his hands. "You can borrow this. See if it sparks any interest."

He smiled with tight lips and put the book under his arm quickly without looking at it. "Thank you."

"Well, at least see what's inside. I could find something else, if you'd prefer."

Hesitantly, he pulled the book from under his arm and cracked the pages open.

Elizabeth pointed at Florence Nightingale's name. "Read that line!"

North snapped the book shut and gave her a steely glare. "Not now."

"Why?" she pushed, even though it wasn't her usual tactic. He'd hurt her feelings, and she needed a good explanation for his sudden rudeness.

He sighed deeply and lowered his voice. "To be frank, I don't read well aloud."

"Oh."

"Yes, so I don't enjoy doing it." He cleared his throat and looked deeply into her eyes as if deciding something. "I'll tell you this, but you must promise not to think less of me."

She frowned. "Of course not. What is it?"

"For as long as I can remember, whenever I try to read, the letters move around on me." He lowered his voice even more. "It's as if I see a page different from everyone else. I understand how words work, but then when I try to read a passage, especially out loud or under pressure, they all melt together or rearrange themselves into the wrong order."

That was not what Elizabeth had been expecting him to say. "My goodness. That sounds quite difficult. I don't know what to say, but I'm so sorry for pushing it on you."

He gave her a half-smile, which made the dimple on his left cheek show. "Not your fault. You didn't know."

Then she remembered the incident on the train, when she had watched him stare at a single page of the newspaper for the duration of the trip. And then it made sense.

"I'm terribly sorry," she said again. "Perhaps I could work with you—"

"No," he blurted. "It's not like that. I don't need to be tutored. Is that what you think I mean?"

Stunned, she stepped back. "I . . . I guess—"

"I should go," he said curtly. He handed the book back to her and saw himself out the door without another word.

Her breath caught in her throat, and she hurried upstairs to her room before her mother could ask her what was wrong.

It shocked her that North couldn't read. How had he made it through school and work as a conductor not being able to read?

He seemed sharp and witty, kind and gracious, so she couldn't imagine it had anything to do with his intelligence. Nevertheless, it was a revelation that made her want to rethink every encounter they'd had.

And even if it reflected a deficit in his mental capacities, that might be something they had in common. Certainly, of a different nature, but it felt familiar. A private detail about his life that he hid from others.

He was a wonderful man, and the truth came over her that she quite liked him. She'd always thought of him as a smart man, and somehow this quirk didn't seem to make North any less intelligent in her eyes. And his encouraging her to go back to the hospital meant more to her than she dared admit. He was right, of course.

And now, she had upset him greatly, just as she realized how much her affections for him were growing.

# CHAPTER SEVENTEEN
## THE HUNT

*Anna*

As Ben packed his things to leave on the hunting trip, Anna remained in the kitchen. It wasn't like them to not speak, but this was their first disagreement where they just couldn't see the other's point of view.

How could he not see how badly she needed the adventure at this moment in her life?

Before he left, he came in and kissed her on the forehead. "I should be back in less than three days. Take good care of yourself, my love. Greta will check in on you."

She made herself smile. She loved him dearly, but she was not pleased with him.

"I love you. More than anything else. And next year, if you want to, you should plan on coming hunting."

"I love you too."

He smiled, seemingly satisfied and gathered his bag and bow.

As she watched him walking away toward the Gallagher house to meet her brother and grandfather, she sat motionless. It would be best to wait until the afternoon before gathering her own things.

She had spoken with Heather, who had agreed to go hunting with her while the men were on their own trip. It felt good to be making secret plans again—exciting. Ben wouldn't be pleased with her, but it was something she simply must do. He would understand eventually.

Hopefully.

When she was sure the hunting party had already traveled south into the forest for miles, Anna grabbed her fully packed bag from the closet and started out toward Heather's house. She didn't need to carry much, because her friend had insisted on carrying their bedding and tent.

The last time she'd been camping with Heather had been when they'd gone salmon fishing with her Duwamish relatives almost two years earlier.

When she knocked on the door, her friend was ready with her own large bag on her back.

"Michael doesn't mind having Pisha by himself for the weekend?" Anna asked.

"They'll be fine. Are you sure Ben doesn't mind you hunting without him?"

"Well played," Anna said, smiling at her friend. "He will understand in time."

Heather put her hand on Anna's shoulder. "I do believe you need this. Let's go."

They walked toward the east, in the direction of Lake Washington. There, they would meet Duwamish friends of Heather's who would take them across the lake to a good hunting place.

Anna took in the beauty of the forest as they walked. She wore the fox fur vest Heather had given her for Christmas the first year they'd known each other. The growing bump of her belly prevented her from closing it completely, but it had been a mild December, and she was already warm from her thick coat and the exercise.

By the time they arrived near the shore of the lake, it was growing dark and cold. The silhouette of a man and a woman next to a large canoe came as a relief.

"*Wiiac*, friends," Heather greeted them. "This is Anna Chambers. Thank you for meeting us."

The man smiled and put out his hand to Anna. "I'm Henry and this is my wife, Ellen."

His English was perfect, and Anna wondered if those were their given names or just what they went by now. They both had dark skin and black hair, and they looked much like Heather, but had graying hair.

"It's wonderful to meet you both."

The woman smiled from where she stood on the shore, holding the end of the canoe. "Let's hurry. It's getting late. We'll take you back to our home tonight, and we can start early tomorrow morning on the other side of the lake. We've seen elk there lately."

Anna grinned. She'd never shot an elk before, and even if they all split the meat, there would be more than enough.

They all took places in the canoe, and it slipped quietly over the dark waters. The moon was full above them, and

Anna knew that Ben would be admiring it at some point that evening as well. Her heart squeezed knowing that he imagined her safe at home, and she hoped she wasn't putting herself into any real danger.

The motion on the water made her more nauseated than she'd expected, and as she stepped off the polished wood onto the shore, she was sick in the tall grasses.

The next morning, they all awoke early before the winter sun had risen. Anna dressed as warmly as possible, knowing they would be outside the entire day and then staying that evening under the stars.

As they set out into the forest, Ellen came up beside her. "When are you expecting your little one?"

"Around the end of April, I believe."

"Wonderful. All our children are grown and have chosen to live on the reservation with the rest of the Duwamish."

Anna nodded. No wonder Heather was close with these folks. They shared her beliefs as well as her blood.

Henry was walking beside Heather, a shotgun strapped to his back. "Will you be visiting the reservation this spring? To speak with your mother?"

Heather nodded and smiled at Anna as she turned around to look at her. "As soon as this baby is safely delivered, I'll leave."

"You're lucky to have such a wise woman to help with your birth. Heather comes from a long line of women who know how to bring babies into this world safely." Ellen put her hand briefly on Anna's forearm, which was covered in layers.

An owl hooted from somewhere above them as the sun began to lighten the horizon. Anna pulled out her mint-soaked handkerchief, as had become her habit. Nothing seemed to be bothering her stomach or her nose at the moment, but those things always came on suddenly. It was better to be ahead of them.

An unfamiliar animal call came from the far edge of the tree line, and Ellen lifted her hand to halt them. They all became still to listen. Henry nodded and pointed slightly to the north, and they marched toward what they hoped was a herd of elk.

It was glorious to be outdoors when the sun rose. Anna could see her breath as a white mist around her face. The crisp air touched the little skin that wasn't protected from the elements, and there was nowhere she'd rather be.

Even holding her bow gave her a sense of comfort. How long had it been since she had done target practice?

Far too long.

Soon, they arrived in a meadow, where Ellen and Henry took positions low in the grass. She and Heather followed suit.

The grass was covered in an icy frost. There still had not been any snowfall, but it almost looked like a wintery scene anyhow. From their lookout, she could see animal footprints in the white of the frozen dew. Some looked small, like rabbits or squirrels, but there were larger tracks that she knew to be elk or deer.

The coldness was a reprieve from her nausea. Heat seemed to intensify smells, and so the lack of it created a wonderful world of very few strong scents. And in that way, her stomach felt better than it had in days. A freshness surrounded her— cold, breezy, and silent.

They waited for hours, only whispering now and then about what they heard or whether they should move to another spot. By midday, Anna's stomach was growling angrily, so she nibbled on the jerky she had tucked away in her coat pocket.

Clouds came overhead in the wintery silence, but neither rain nor snow fell upon them. It was difficult to tell when dusk came because the darkness had been creeping in for some time.

"Shall we head back to our house, or would you like to set up camp?" Henry asked in a low tone.

"Let's stay out here," Anna said quickly. "I don't mind at all."

He nodded and motioned for them to follow. They found a flat area some ways off with a tree covering that would do well.

She began to set up her tent while Ellen and Heather searched for sticks for a fire.

Later, they sat around a blazing flame eating bread, cheese, and jam.

"How have things been in the city?" Ellen asked Heather.

She frowned before answering. "Sometimes I'm happy, but there have been problems now and then. For the most part, it's the right choice for me. Although I certainly wouldn't mind moving out to this area where you are. How have you been liking it out here?"

"According to the government, we don't own any land here, so it's only a matter of time before someone else claims it," Henry replied, stoking the fire with a stick. "I'm afraid we'll have to move on soon."

"You can move into town," Heather said. "I would be delighted to have you both closer, and you'd still be on true Duwamish land."

"Yes, we've considered that," Ellen said, wrapping her coat tighter around her thin shoulders. "We're getting older, and it would be nice to settle down in a community. I'm just not sure how welcome we'll be."

Heather grinned. "I'll speak with Michael about you

building on our land. It could be a good distance from our place, perhaps, so you're comfortable."

Ellen seemed more interested in the prospect than Henry, but both smiled and thanked her for the kind offer.

"We should get to sleep as soon as possible. I'd like to be back to the meadow before sunrise tomorrow," Henry said as he stood.

Anna stayed awhile near the fire, lying on her back to admire the sky. The North star and the Big Dipper were her favorites. She thought of Ben's poem, "The Stars Out Here Are Free," and she felt the truth of it deep inside. Surely, he had to understand the way she felt.

Early the next morning, Ellen popped her head into Anna and Heather's tent to quietly rouse them.

They packed up their camp entirely, as they would be heading home that evening, with or without a kill. Anna was sure that Ben would be home that day or the next, and she wanted to beat him there. She was going to tell him the truth, but it would be easier if she told him face to face instead of him reading the note she'd left.

One more day of freedom—one more chance to shoot.

They moved slowly, stepping quietly over the frozen earth. Before the sun rose, they were in position near the meadow.

After a few minutes in the foggy moonlight, two elk appeared in the center of the meadow. One with his head down and the other alert, watching the horizon.

Henry pointed to Anna.

Did he want her to be the one to shoot?

It wasn't worth the risk of speaking, even in a whisper. She pointed to herself and then her bow with a question in her expression.

He nodded.

With a shaky but silent exhale, she leaned behind a thick tree trunk to rise to her knees, then readied an arrow.

Slowly, she moved her face from behind the tree so she could see the elk. For a moment, they both had their heads down to eat, but then one lifted his head in the opposite direction.

Anna took her shot.

Just as the arrow reached the elk, he turned his body toward them. What would have been a perfect placement ended up piercing the animal's backside.

But just as quickly, Ellen loosed another arrow that landed squarely in the back of the head of the majestic elk. He fell immediately as his partner fled.

The commotion of the animal hitting the ground, and the other's pounding hoofs, made Anna's heart race.

They'd done it.

It felt surreal, but the fact that it had truly happened made her chest swell with pride. She wished her arrow would have landed true, but some things couldn't be controlled, especially in the wild.

It had been a team effort, which made it all the sweeter, if she chose to look at it that way. A new bond between her and these new friends.

As the fog lifted and the sky turned a lighter gray above them, Heather and Ellen carved into the meat with impressively sized knives.

True to Greta's warning, the warm, pungent organs spilling out into the grass made Anna's stomach turn immediately. She ran as far as she could to heave, but it poured out of her only a few steps away, and she narrowly avoided stepping in it.

"Go for a walk, Anna," Heather said kindly. "Henry, would you go with her so she doesn't get lost?"

Anna turned back to her friend feeling a little insulted, but Heather was right. She'd never been in these woods, and she was in no shape to be thoughtful about finding her way around.

Henry offered his arm, but Anna shook her head with a smile. "I'm fine now, thank you. I would love to walk with you, though. Where shall we go?"

"There's a creek just ahead. Let's see if we can collect some water for the group."

She nodded, grateful they could do something helpful while the other women did the most difficult work.

Once they were out of sight from the others, Henry asked, "Is Heather doing as well as she says? Ellen and I worry about her sometimes."

"I can't say she's perfectly happy, but I think she's more satisfied than she'd be if she were living at the reservation. She feels the same as you do about staying on Duwamish land."

He nodded, concern still etched in his brow. "Ellen was good friends with Heather's mother once. I hope Heather and her mother can reconcile when she visits this spring."

"I hope so too. At least she has Michael and Pisha with her. She'll always have them—and you and Ellen."

When they arrived at the creek, it was crystal clear, so they filled their skins and canteens with the cool water.

After the meat and organs had been split and wrapped, Ellen returned home while Henry took Anna and Heather back across the lake in the canoe.

"It was good to see you as always, Heather," he said as they reached the shore. "Please write to us or visit, and let us know how your time on the reservation goes."

"I will."

They said their goodbyes and then walked briskly to make it home by nightfall.

Anna felt satisfied with the hunting trip, and it had eased her need for adventure and contributing. But by the time she reached her house, she was shaking with nerves.

Would Ben already be there?

# CHAPTER EIGHTEEN
## THROUGH HIS EYES

*Elizabeth | January 1892*

A few days after the embarrassing encounter at dinner, Elizabeth decided she must apologize to Mr. Bailey—North, as she could call him now. He hadn't visited her since then. She still had so many questions, but she knew for sure and certain that she didn't want him to distance himself from her.

She knew he spent Monday mornings in his office at the train station, and so she surprised him with a visit. With a basket of chocolate muffins and a dried bouquet of mint tied with white ribbon, she set out to the station.

As she strolled in the chilly morning, she wrapped her mink cloak around her tightly. She knew he had feelings for her, but their last encounter felt like a bad sign—an omen. Perhaps he was finished with her, and she might expect a letter saying so shortly. Although he'd promised not to break their courtship with something as rude as a letter. But maybe he would be his humorous self and send a telegram.

When she arrived, she had to ask around to find him. Tucked in a small corner of the depot, she found him staring up at a map of Washington on the wall of his office.

"Good morning," she mumbled.

He turned to look at her with surprise.

"Oh. Hello, Elizabeth. I'm sorry I haven't . . . I mean—" He cleared his throat and folded his arms over his chest.

She didn't know how to read his greeting. Was he still cross with her? Or did he want to pretend nothing had happened?

Did he even still want to court her?

"Do come in and have a seat. Unless you're still angry with me for not taking your book, that is."

"I wasn't upset. I thought I upset *you*." She set her basket down and folded her arms across her chest, mimicking his defensive stance.

He shook his head but said nothing.

So, was she forgiven?

Had she even done anything that needed forgiving?

"I'm sorry about trying to force my book upon you—"

"There's no need for an apology, Elizabeth. Your intentions were kind."

"Are you uncomfortable that you told me about your reading habits?"

He finally uncrossed his arms and sat at his desk. "I suppose I'd prefer you didn't know, but if we'd like to keep getting to know each other, this kind of thing will come up, won't it?"

She nodded nervously and took a seat as well. Her secrets

weren't anything she wanted to share unless she absolutely must.

"Do you think less of me?" he asked.

"Of course not. Not at all."

He grinned. "Good."

She certainly liked that he was willing to be open about something that most people would be embarrassed about. Not that he had shared it willingly, but now that she knew, she could see that he didn't really mind it about himself. She could use that kind of forgiving perspective about herself.

Should she tell him anything private about herself? It was far too soon, surely. Having difficulties with reading was one thing, but having a life's dream of staying out of the insane asylum was another.

What might he think of her if he knew?

She bit the inside of her cheek and avoided his eyes, although she could sense he was watching her.

"I fancy you, Elizabeth Grayson," he said with an intense gaze. "I like the way you seem to think of everything, and that your mind is always working, even if you won't always share your thoughts. And I admire your desire to help people. I think you might be too good for me."

She was dizzy from his words.

Could he really believe all those things about her?

If she let herself, she could see how it was all true—all the things he'd said about her. Every part of her brain wanted to disagree, to hate who she was.

But when she saw herself through his eyes, she saw a different person. Or maybe it was the real her.

His kindness was a relief from the way she felt about herself.

"I don't know what to say, North."

"I like hearing you say my name."

She could feel the blush that came over her cheeks, but she made herself look into his eyes, and his fierce look did not disappoint. He wasn't going to kiss her, was he?

He reached for a muffin and took a bite. "These are good. And what do I do with the dried mint? Sprinkle it on top?"

Elizabeth laughed and his humor dissipated the tension. He knew just when to break the serious feel in their conversations.

"You can make tea with it."

"Ah, that sounds right," he said with a wink. "Well, can I make you some tea? I can probably find a kettle to boil somewhere—"

"No, but thank you. I should let you get back to your work. Still, I'm glad I came by."

"As am I."

He showed her to the door of his office and looked down at her lips before nodding graciously and turning on his heel.

She breathed a sigh of relief, but there was a disappointment just beneath the surface. A kiss might have been nice.

And with that, Elizabeth felt that all was right again in the world.

Except that she was falling in love.

# CHAPTER NINETEEN
## A PARTY FOR ST. VALENTINE'S DAY

*Anna | February 1892 | The Seventh Month*

en's reaction to her secret hunting trip had been mild. Anna had expected some type of explosive argument, but when he had arrived home just hours after she had, there hadn't been much left to be angry about. She was home safe, their trip had gone well, and she was apologetic.

He hadn't been happy about it, but he'd forgiven her, as she'd hoped he would.

But there was a certain air to the way he treated her now, and that had been going on for a couple weeks. Now, there was a sort of separation between them.

She didn't like it at all.

Anna sighed, looking down at the invitation in her hand. It was silky smooth and smelled of lavender. She untied the satin ribbon and broke the seal, but she already knew who had sent it.

Emily had been talking about throwing a small Valentine's Day party for weeks. A proper party, that is. The only guests invited were Anna and Ben, as well as Heather and Michael, but that would not stop her from creating all the luscious, detailed aspects of a traditional Saint Valentine's Day party.

Heather had asked if she could borrow one of Anna's dresses, as she hadn't bought any fancy ones yet that were fit for an event.

The afternoon of the party, Heather arrived looking nervous.

"Come in! Hello, Pisha. Are you coming to the party as well?" Anna asked. Emily loved children, but the party would not be the kind that children were invited to, for propriety and the fine china, for heaven's sake.

"No, your grandmother watch me," the girl said shyly.

"Mrs. Gallagher is her name. And in English, you'll say she *will* watch me because it will happen in the future," Heather corrected.

"And what a fine time you will have with her," Anna said, taking Pisha's hand as they entered. "Did you know my grandmother makes the best cookies in all of Seattle? Maybe the entire world . . ."

Pisha laughed. "My great grandmother made the best salmon."

Anna remembered Heather's grandmother, Kiyotsa, fondly.

Heather seemed quick to move on from the subject. "I'm sure you'll have a lovely time with Mrs. Gallagher. Why don't you go find Comma?"

Pisha ran to the back door, where the dog was curled up on

a rug.

"Now," she said, turning to Anna. "What shall I wear to this fine party Emily has invited us to?"

Anna laughed. "She'll make it as fancy as she can, but really, it will just be the six of us, so there's no pressure to look a certain way."

"I know, but I thought it would be a treat for Michael. To dress like a town lady for the party. Do you think he'll like it?"

That made Anna think about Ben. She paused to wonder if he would think her pretty at the party, or even really enjoy her company. It was getting hard to tell, but it was probably just her emotions going awry.

"I think he adores you, so yes, of course he will."

They searched through Anna's closet and found a dark red dress with white satin trim. The back closed with woven ribbons that tied in a bow, so it could conform to Heather's unique figure.

"Would you like to wear all the underthings as well?" Anna asked doubtfully.

"I don't see why not."

With a nod, she pulled out a corset and petticoats. "All right, but I'll remind you later that you wanted this."

It was Heather's turn to laugh. "It's just for fun. I'm not buying a whole new wardrobe or anything."

"I know. I'm just teasing." Anna smiled as she handed over the underthings. "I'll step out while you get these on, and when I come back in, I'll help lace up the corset."

Outside her own bedroom door, she thought about the first time she had put on a fancy dress and gone out. She had been a young lady of thirteen, going out to dinner with her grandfather, Greta, and Levi. The thing she remembered most was that she felt like a princess.

"I'm ready," Heather called from inside the room.

"And how would you like to do your hair?" Anna asked as she returned to help lace up the corset.

"Something besides my usual braids?"

"Whatever you'd like. I'm not an expert with styling hair, but I'll do my best to sweep it up. It's too bad June's not here."

"Yes, I thought of her this morning. Have you received any news from her lately?"

Anna sighed. "She sent me a letter at Christmas. They are all doing well. And they're hoping to come visit again in the summer. She can't wait to meet my baby, of course."

With a delicate hand, she pulled the dress over Heather's head and helped her lace the back and situate it just right over the petticoats. Once she was fully dressed, Anna stood her friend in front of the mirror.

"My goodness," Heather said, eyes wide. "If my skin wasn't so dark, it would almost look as if I belonged here in this town."

Anna frowned. She couldn't imagine what it must be like to live the truth of that discrimination.

"Oh, Heather! Please don't think that way. I don't—"

"I know," Heather replied with a dismissive wave of her hand. "*You* don't, but there are so many who do. Does it surprise you that the thought crosses my mind?"

"No, I suppose not."

"You don't need to feel sorry for me. I've chosen to be here. Let's fix my hair."

Anna nodded without another word, although she wanted to address the issue. She knew it was hard for her friend to live in town, but it was also a statement she was making. This *was* her land.

She brushed Heather's long dark hair and twisted it up

with a pearl barrette.

When they came down the stairs, Pisha gasped at the vision of her mother.

"Beautiful, Mama!"

"Thank you, dear. Let's get you over to the Gallaghers so your father and I can go to the party."

"I want to come too," Pisha said with a pout.

"Not yet, my darling. We'll have a fine tea party tomorrow afternoon with your doll. How does that sound?"

They said their temporary farewells until they would see each other again at the party that evening.

Later, in the carriage on the way to Emily and Levi's house, Anna glanced at Ben as he watched the trees go by out the small window.

"Michael is going to be surprised, isn't he?"

"I'd say so. But I suppose he thinks his wife is beautiful no matter what she wears. He probably prefers her without clothes."

"Ben!" She blushed, laughing.

He winked and reached for her hand. It brought a huge sense of relief over her. He still adored her.

On her lap were the two cards they were bringing, as requested. Emily had said to address them simply "To my cavalier" and "To my lady." But their own names were hidden inside the envelopes on each corner of the respective notes. This was an important part, Emily had assured them.

The cards were to be original, or at least contain a quotation from a notable poet. Although Emily had encouraged them to write their own rhymes—valiant or silly, anything would do as long as it was well penned.

When they pulled up to the house, Emily opened the front door and waved in greeting. She wore a white lace wrap over her pink dress. A double ruffle of lace joined at the waist with a sash tied in a bow.

Inside, they found a white bag in the hall where they were to deposit the Valentine's Day cards.

A tray of popcorn balls made with molasses was out, and Levi poured wine into stemmed goblets.

"You look lovely, sister," he said, smiling his gap-toothed grin at Anna. "You clean up alright, Ben, but I've seen better."

"You've seen me looking quite terrible, haven't you? I'd say this is as good as it gets." Ben laughed and patted Levi on the shoulder.

Anna smiled at her husband, who was far handsomer than her brother. At least in her opinion.

"We have butterscotch and chocolate cream candies," Emily said, beaming.

Candles were lit in every corner of the sitting room, with evergreen boughs along the fireplace. She had displayed a vase full of holly and more evergreen branches on the mantel. Peacock feathers adorned the vase—Emily had planned each detail with exquisite care.

When Heather and Michael arrived, a silence fell over the room.

"Heather, you look stunning!" Emily exclaimed, rushing toward her. "How lovely. I'm honored you dressed up so much for my party."

She kissed Heather on the cheek and smiled in greeting to Michael.

"What a beautiful lady you have on your arm, sir," Emily said.

Michael grinned and handed her their cards. "I suppose I should give these to you?"

Emily picked up the white bag and extended her hands

with the top open.

"Yes, just drop them in the bag." Then she turned to address everyone. "For pairing off for supper, I've written slips of paper, each with a lady's name on it. Each man will draw a name and then escort that lady to dinner."

Anna laughed. "Isn't that tradition for parties with single guests?"

"Don't spoil it, Anna!" Emily said with a hurt look. "We're all happily married to our valentine, so let's just have a little fun, shall we?"

"Yes, of course. Keep going."

Emily nodded with a grin and continued. "After you've drawn a lady's name, gentlemen, you will serve her supper like a true cavalier."

Ben lifted his eyebrows and smiled at Anna. Then he whispered in her ear, "I might have to fight for you, my lady."

She laughed and kissed his cheek. Then she put her hand on her belly as she felt a small kick. What a wonder to behold. She was grateful for each movement, proof of the life inside her. Even when the kicks poked sharply at her ribs.

Michael was the first to put his hand into the bag of names, from which he pulled out Anna's name.

He came over to her and offered his arm, which she took. "Thank you, sir. I'd be honored to join you at the table."

Ben frowned and then exaggerated his disappointment with a dramatic sigh, which made Emily giggle.

Levi drew Heather's name, which left Ben to escort Emily.

When they arrived in the dining room, Anna's grandfather stood at the head of the table with a skullcap, long cloak, and his white beard finely combed. Behind his right shoulder, he held the sack of cards.

He whispered to Anna, "Do I look as ridiculous as I feel?"

She grinned at him, then glanced at Emily, who was beaming.

"And this is our very own Saint Valentine!"

Even Levi raised his eyebrows in amusement. Emily must have kept the delicious secret all to herself.

As each man seated the lady he had escorted, Anna winked at her grandfather, who cleared his throat before speaking.

"It's my grave honor to present the cards this evening," he said, opening the sack he held. "I'm to auction off each card, one by one. You can offer the promise of a dance, a serving of your dessert tonight, a compliment, a favor, and so on."

"That sounds fun," Heather said, much to Emily's delight.

"The first card says 'To my cavalier.' Do we have any bids for this card?"

No one spoke until Ben clapped his hands together. "I'll offer a dance for that fine card."

"I'll raise you a favor," said Levi with a playfully challenging look. He smiled at Emily, who was across the room, and she blushed.

"I'll offer a genuine compliment," Ben replied, crossing his arms over his large chest.

"Sold!"

Oscar handed the card to him, and he used his knife to slit the envelope open.

"Ahh, from the lovely Mrs. Gallagher." Ben gave Emily a gracious nod. "It says 'To the cavalier: Roses are red, violets are blue, may the joy of the party go home with you.' No doubt it will. Thank you, Emily."

"What's your compliment?" Anna asked.

"Well, that one's easy," he said, turning to face Emily. "My dear sister-in-law, this is the finest Valentine's Day party I have ever attended. My compliments to the knowledgeable and gracious hostess."

Everyone clapped softly, and Emily blushed deeply. "Thank you so much, Ben. It was a delight to put together."

Anna grinned, knowing that her husband always had thoughtful compliments on hand. Her grandfather reached into the sack and pulled out another card.

"This one says 'To the lady.'"

"I'll offer a dance," Emily said, eyes sparkling.

Anna clapped her hands together with an idea. "I'll bid a plate of cookies."

"Anyone else?" her grandfather said slowly, winking at Heather.

She smiled softly. "I'll offer my dessert this evening."

"Heather wins this round!" He handed the card to her, and she opened it quickly.

"It says,

To the lady:

Love is not love
Which alters when it alteration finds,
Or bends with the remover to remove;
O no! it is an ever-fixed mark
That looks on tempests and is never shaken.

By William Shakespeare

(Levi)

Heather turned to face him. "Thank you for the lovely poem. I know it's true for you."

Levi's face turned a light shade of pink, and he smiled across the table at Emily.

"Let's do one more for now, and then we'll let the cavaliers serve dinner to the ladies," Emily said.

"All right, this one is 'To the lady' again."

"I'll offer a large plate of popcorn balls and chocolate-creams to take home with you," Emily said.

"But I can offer a compliment," Anna said, smiling at her grandfather.

"I will have to give this one to Emily," he said, winking at Anna.

Emily took the card and gingerly opened the envelope, which was sealed with golden wax. "My, this sure looks lovely. It says,

To the lady:

Like a lady's ringlets brown,
Flow thy silken ears adown
Either side demurely,
Of thy silver-suited breast
Shining out from all the rest
Of thy body purely."

Ben stifled a laugh behind his hand, then cleared his throat.

"Those are lovely words, Michael. I'm not sure what they mean, but I thank you for the lovely card."

Ben looked as if he couldn't hold back his thoughts any longer. "They might confuse you a little because Elizabeth Barrett Browning wrote them to her dog."

Levi erupted in laughter, and Michael followed suit. A

blush covered Emily's face, and Anna immediately felt for her.

"My apologies, Emily," Michael said, putting his hands in the air defensively. "I thought it would be funny. I didn't mean for you specifically to get it."

"It's quite all right. It's always good to keep a dose of humor at a party. I'll have your plate of desserts ready before you leave this evening," she said, not looking him in the eye.

"Let's serve these ladies dinner. Shall we, gentlemen?" Levi said, standing to his feet. He walked over to the dining cart against the wall and lifted a tray with three silver platters covered with tops.

While they ate, Emily seemed to shake her embarrassment. "Anna, how have you been feeling? You're coming up on your true confinement, I believe."

"I'm well, thank you. And I don't truly plan to keep to the house—maybe toward the very end."

Emily swallowed and patted her perfectly clean lips with her napkin. "Some of the older ladies on the library association mentioned that you would be absent in the next few months."

Ben chimed in. "That seems silly."

"I don't think that'll be necessary," Anna said, her heart pounding.

Emily nodded slowly. "I'll put in a friendly word for you. But speak with them. They did mention that it would be unseemly to have a woman at the meeting in your advanced condition. I'm sorry, I thought you should know. Of course, I think it's perfectly respectful for you to come—"

"My goodness, it's as if Peter himself plans to run the meeting." Anna cleared her throat. "It's fine. I won't come. I wouldn't want to offend the fragile natures of those fine ladies."

Ben crossed his arms over his chest from across the table, and Anna knew he wanted to comfort her with a touch.

"I'm sorry, Anna," Emily said, regret in her tone.

"Have you heard anything new of Peter?" Heather asked, leaning into the table toward her.

"No. Nothing." Anna sighed. "I don't even know why I mentioned his name."

Ben cleared his throat. "I've seen signs for him around town. It's just a matter of time, I believe."

And then he quickly changed the subject by asking Michael about work at the mill.

Inside, Anna seethed. It was ridiculous that the association thought it inappropriate for her to come *sit* at a meeting. She wasn't expecting the baby for two full months. Sure, her shape had rounded and blossomed, but there was nothing unseemly about it.

She thought about going anyway and arguing but then thought better of it. She might just end up embarrassing herself and her grandfather. To these older ladies, the library association was their world, and she was just a young lady joining in on the society event.

She would be unable to do this one small thing, even though it required virtually no physical exertion. All because she was a mother-to-be. All the unfairness seemed to crush her at once.

It was at that moment that she recalled Dr. Evans' words about women being physically incapable of things men are, and she wanted to scream.

And then she remembered who she was. She would definitely go to the next meeting. Compared with Peter holding a knife to her on the mountain, those old ladies were nothing to fear.

# CHAPTER TWENTY
## TOMATOES

*Elizabeth | March 1892*

There was something about routine that made Elizabeth feel like the world was all right. After she made tea, she watched the hummingbirds outside the kitchen window. They flitted from the feeder to the hydrangeas and back again. She could empathize with their indecisiveness, their restless spirits. There was a grace to their speed.

The spring equinox had come and gone, and with it, a new sense of contentment had arrived. As the end of the month neared, she looked forward to warmer months ahead.

With a sigh, she picked up the breakfast tray she had prepared for her mother, who'd fallen ill with a terrible spring cold the day before and refused to get out of her bed. Elizabeth didn't mind taking care of her one bit. She had nothing else to do besides play the violin and read nursing manuals she might never even put into practice.

Just as she left the kitchen, a knock sounded at the door. She set the tray back down and hurried to the door, checking her reflection in the hall mirror. Much to her surprise, she looked happy, although her nerves had maintained a stronger presence throughout the winter and spring than she'd ever imagined.

Her light blue eyes twinkled back at her, and her blond hair wasn't perfect but still mostly in the braid from the day before.

When she opened the door, North was standing before her wearing a brown button-up shirt and trousers. Trays and buckets surrounded him, and a thin layer of dirt covered his hands.

"Morning, Elizabeth," he said. "Is your mother home? I've brought her tomatoes."

"Good morning," she replied. "She is here, but she's ill. I'm sorry—what poor timing. She was so looking forward to planting your tomatoes in her garden."

North wiped some dirt off on his trousers and smiled warmly. "Well, I don't think I'd like to bring all this stuff back home. Would she mind if we planted them without her?"

"A little, but she'll live." She chuckled. "Let me run breakfast up to her room, and I'll meet you at the back of the house. You'll see the garden."

She closed the door, heart pounding. He certainly seemed happy to see her, as always.

When she joined him in the garden, she surveyed the things he'd brought.

"What a collection," she said, glancing around at everything strewn about the grass.

"Well, yes, seedlings and seeds too. But it's kind of late in the season already, so I wanted to give you some of my seedlings I planted indoors a few weeks ago. They're ready to be transplanted."

"Thank you." The little green plants looked so uniform in their spacing that it made her sigh with satisfaction. A small pleasure.

He glanced around the backyard with an impressed lift of his eyebrows. "Lovely garden. What area do you think she wants the tomatoes planted in?"

"I think my mother is so delighted to have them that she won't mind where they go. How about over here?"

He strolled past her toward the area in which she pointed, and as he did, she caught a scent of him. Something like the smell of an ice-cold creek in the forest. Their shoulders brushed as she turned to lead the way, and a tingle went down her spine.

A lost seagull came to land on the grass, and she shooed it away, happy to have a task to do besides following North around the garden.

"We sure appreciate all this," she said, gesturing to the supplies he'd brought. Small clay pots with seedlings, a flour sack full of soil, a small tin pail of seeds, and a bag of something she couldn't identify but which did not smell good.

She'd never been very interested in gardening, or very good at it. She resisted the urge to feel stupid as he dove in.

"First, we'll mix in some aged horse droppings into your garden. Don't worry, they're a few years old, and it's practically dirt now. Then we'll plant the seeds. These little ones will be hungry when they sprout."

She laughed. "Little ones?"

He grinned, clearly pleased that he amused her. "They're my babies. Most important rule about babies—feed them."

"Do you have a lot of experience with babies?" she asked with a teasing lift of her eyebrows.

"I don't think I've ever even held a real baby," North said matter-of-factly, although she sensed a feeling of loss in his tone.

"You don't have any extended family or relatives around? No babies to celebrate every now and then?" she asked as she shoveled spades full of the dirt previously identified as horse droppings.

"I do not," he replied. "Now, we'll plant the seeds."

"What about the *little ones* you brought?" she asked with just the hint of a smile.

"Ahh, yes. We'll do those last, if the weather allows."

She looked up at the low clouds. A thick spring rain seemed imminent.

"I'll have you put the seeds in yourself. There's something about touching them with your own fingers that connects you with them. It makes you want to care for them as they grow."

"Are you teasing me?" she asked

"Am I?" he replied with a playfully challenging look.

"Perhaps you should have waited for my mother to help you with these. I'm afraid I just don't have the bond to the earth like you do."

"Well, there's always time to remedy that," he said with a wink.

She sighed and opened her palm, and he lifted the cup of seeds. With one hand, he poured, and the other he put under her hand, probably to make sure none of the tiny seeds slipped through her fingers. His palm was warm beneath hers, and she liked the way his touch made her feel

—calm, and without thought, the same as when she played the violin.

With a brain like hers, it was hard to be without thought. Some fear, worry, or doubt always played on a loop.

She wasn't sure if it came from the tactile pleasure of having earth in her fingernails and seeds in her hands, or just being outside, or North's touch. But it all proved soothing, and she couldn't remember the last time she'd been so at ease.

With a twig, North made indents in the earth in a straight line along the garden row. Elizabeth sprinkled a couple of seeds in each spot.

To her, it seemed like such a slow process. That's why she never enjoyed helping her mother in the garden with the mint. She could easily pick up mint or tomatoes at their own grocer and eat them immediately. But growing them from seed took months. The delay usually infuriated her, but the way North seemed to enjoy it intrigued her.

Things take time, which is hard to remember. Things that *matter* take time, and maybe the slow progression makes the thing more enjoyable once it comes to fruition.

"Do you have a watering can?" he asked, breaking the silence.

"Yes, I'll fill it." She stood, brushing the dirt from her skirts.

She returned with a full watering can.

"Next year, you and your mother can start seeds growing indoors on your windowsill in February."

"So, we'll be on our own next year?" she asked, as coy as she could manage.

"Assuming you've had enough of me," he replied, his cheeks turning pink. "And, once the seeds sprout and grow their first set of true leaves, they'll need some love."

"Some love?"

He stood and took the watering can from her. "Yes. If they were outside like the ones we just planted, the wind would blow them around a bit. That's what makes them grow strong, hearty stems, which they'll need when they're bigger. So, to replicate the wind, you'll just blow on them a couple times a day like this."

He leaned down and blew a soft breath over one of the small plants he had brought over, as if he were blowing out a candle. His lips were full and more rose-colored than she'd noticed before. She pressed her own lips together tightly, wondering how his lips would feel against hers.

"And then, another thing that helps is just rubbing a finger along the stem." He put one finger to a stem and ran it up and down the spine, from soil to the first set of leaves. "See the little spiny hairs? They sense things for the plant. So, if you give them a little resistance and gentle jostling, they learn to get tough."

Elizabeth swallowed and nodded. "So, with a pretty light touch? It doesn't hurt them, right?"

"Really lightly," he said, reaching for her hand.

He ran his finger along the back of it gently from knuckles to wrist with a touch that was soft but steady. The hairs on her arms stood up.

"I see," she said, not pulling her hand away. He looked into her eyes with a smile slowly growing on his lips.

When he finally pulled his hand away, he said, "Calling you Elizabeth seems nearly as formal as calling you Miss Grayson. Do you go by anything shorter? Beth or Eliza?"

She couldn't help but smile at him, even as her heart raced from the recent touch of his hands.

"My family has always just called me Elizabeth." She felt a

blush coming, but she wasn't sure why. Maybe the familiarity with which he was already looking at her.

"Can I call you Liz?"

She laughed. "That's awfully short, but it sounds nice."

"North is short."

"That's true. Liz is pleasant. I think I should like it coming out of your mouth."

Then, the first drop of rain splashed on her. And in true spring rain fashion, the next drops came quickly as the sky darkened.

"Well, Liz," he said with a wink. "I think this is just the beginning of it."

Just as he said it, the wind picked up and knocked over one of his small pots with a seedling in it. He ran to it at once.

Thick raindrops started beating down harder, and the wooden chimes above the back door jostled in the wind.

"We need to get these tomato plants out of the heavy rain," North said.

Most of the little plants were already bent over to the side, with splatters of dirt all over them, and they picked each one up to move them inside.

With their arms full and the rain coming down around them, they tracked water into the house and into the kitchen. They lined them up on the windowsill, and North brushed the dirt away from the leaves. Then he patted down the soil, adjusting the stems so they stood perfectly upright.

Elizabeth shivered from the sudden drop in temperature, her wet clothes still dripping rainwater onto the kitchen floor.

"They'll be alright, won't they?" she asked, running a finger gently along a stem.

He nodded and moved closer to her, then, with a soft

laugh, he brushed his hands against his pants to rub the mud off.

The rain had plastered his hair onto his head. He ran a hand through it and flopped it to the side. Then he took the same hand and brushed her hair away from her wet forehead. The touch of his fingers against her skin gave her a tingling sensation, and she smiled nervously. He smiled back and leaned forward, pressing his lips to hers.

It was soft and nothing like she thought a first kiss would be. She'd always imagined anxiety coloring the experience, or that she'd worry about what she looked like. But as she stood there, soaked to the bone with dirt on her hands, her mind was rapturously calm as his lips moved against hers. One of his hands rested on her shoulder and slid down her arm to her elbow. Then he pulled her closer.

By the time he released her, she remembered where she was and looked around her house apprehensively. They were still alone.

He searched her eyes. She looked down and smiled shyly, then glanced back up at him.

"You are a delight," he whispered. "And I should go."

But he paused before leaving. "Will you do me a favor, Liz?"

She nodded without thinking about what it could be. His presence and his voice put her at such ease, it was hard to imagine that anything he might request wouldn't be in her best interest.

"Go by the hospital tomorrow and see if they need any volunteers. Can't become a nurse by taking care of tomatoes," he said with a wink.

Elizabeth was speechless. She'd been wanting to go back, but every time she tried, the scene of blood flashed in her mind. But he was right, and it was good to have someone encouraging her to do what she dreamed of doing, no matter how difficult it was.

"I will," she said.

After she'd walked him to the door and said a soft goodbye, she laid some towels over the kitchen floor and started water boiling for a bath. Her heart soared from the affection he'd shown her, and her nerves danced with anticipation of possibly going back to the hospital.

# CHAPTER TWENTY-ONE
## THE HAVEN

*Anna | March 1892 | The Eighth Month*

"Are you sure you're ready for this?" Ben asked as their carriage reached the library building.

Anna put a hand to her swelling belly and smiled. "Oh yes. It ought to be fun, don't you think?"

"I only wish I could see their faces. But alas, I must go to work. You can tell me all about it at dinner this evening."

He kissed her softly and then helped her out of the carriage.

Before he let go of her hand, he pulled her close. "I'm sorry I didn't agree to you coming on the hunting trip with us."

Anna froze. It was the first time they had spoken of it since the day he'd returned.

"It's alright. I shouldn't have gone against your wishes. That's not how we are together."

"I understand now why you did."

And with that, he stepped back into the carriage with a charming smile.

It was good to have his support. And good to know that their love was solid. She took a deep breath and climbed the stairs to the fourth floor where the library meeting was to be held.

Then she paused to catch her breath. She got winded so easily lately, and it wouldn't do for her to be heaving as she entered.

Emily had already warned her that the ladies didn't want her to come to any more meetings, and she knew they would disapprove with how far along her condition had advanced. But it wasn't as if she was incapable of sitting in a meeting and sharing her opinions on the workings of the library.

She opened the door wide and waltzed in, making no effort to appear smaller than she was.

There were two gasps and then the room went silent. Emily waved at her bashfully from the table of refreshments.

An older woman tutted at Anna as she walked by and then decided to ignore her.

When Anna reached Emily's side, she saw her grandfather already seated and trying to stifle a laugh. He disguised it by coughing into his handkerchief.

The meeting went smoothly despite a few odd looks given to Anna, and when it was over, a single old woman came up to her.

"You ought to be at home, young lady. You know better."

"Are you worried that I'm contagious?" Anna asked, a twinkle in her eye.

The woman huffed and turned on her heel.

❧

ON THE LAST day of April, Anna wondered if the baby might never come.

She had created an outdoor haven for herself right in her own backyard that had saved her in these final weeks. There were spring flowers and young trees, and often when she sat motionless for a spell, squirrels and bunnies would visit her. The flowers and small bird bath she'd set up seemed to delight the birds, and so gay chirping filled the air.

Her favorite thing to do was to rest in a reclining wooden chair with pillows from inside, sipping on water with slices of lemon. To be outdoors gave her spirit life, and she often went shoeless, letting her bare feet sink into the soft grasses and dirt below.

Between reading, thinking, and brief naps, an entire afternoon might fly by where she felt truly happy and not at all confined to the house. She came to realize that even through the hardships of a tough pregnancy, she could still find joy in her everyday life. She'd made peace with the ill timing of her pregnancy and promised herself that as soon as the baby arrived, she could do nearly anything she wanted to.

As she sat with her eyes closed in her oasis, she heard footsteps coming toward her. Heather, but she was without Pisha this time.

"I'm so glad you came. Have a seat and relax with me."

"It looks lovely. I'd be happy to," Heather replied, putting a cushion on the back of a wooden chair. "Pisha is home with Michael for her afternoon nap. I hope she never grows out of that, but I'm afraid that's coming soon."

"How often do babies nap?" Anna asked.

Should she already know this?

Heather smiled. "It's up to you. And up to them, really. They sleep quite a lot, though, especially at the beginning."

Anna put a hand to her full-sized belly and sighed. "Any day now. The suspense is something I didn't realize would be so thought consuming."

"You can't rush it, of course. Especially not with your first."

"Well, I so appreciate you waiting to leave until I have the baby. But I can't wait to hear all about your trip once you return. Are you getting excited to speak with your mother? Nervous?"

Heather sighed. "I suppose since Pisha isn't here, I can speak more freely about it than I usually do. Do you remember Lana from when you came salmon fishing with us?"

Anna nodded. She could recall Heather's cousin in vivid detail. The woman wore shell earrings, and her knee-length skirt showed off what had looked like brown paintings on her legs. "She was kind to me, I remember."

"Yes, Lana is good. It was she who responded to the letter I wrote my mom."

"So, did your mother refuse to respond, or did she ask Lana to write you?"

Heather shrugged. "I'm unsure. But my mother hasn't spoken with me since I remained behind when they moved to the reservation across the bay. So, the fact that she is requesting for me to come at all is surprising."

"Indeed. Well, I hope the two of you can reconcile, if that is what you're hoping for," Anna said, trying to read her friend's face.

Heather looked up with a small smile. "That would make

me happy, but I believe it is out of my control. I will speak with her, but she'll never convince me to live there, if that's what she's still trying to do."

"So the rift between you two all started because you wanted to remain in Seattle when they moved?"

"I wanted to remain on Duwamish land. They moved to Suquamish land where the government told them to go. But that is not our land."

"Right." Anna bit her lip.

"My mother thinks I have abandoned my people, but I think that they have abandoned our ancestral land. She also hates that I married a white man, but that came after. She does not approve, but I've never cared about that." Heather grinned. "So, whenever we visited our people—my grandmother, Pisha, and I—my mother would only let Pisha near her. Of course, she adores her, but she wouldn't speak with Kiyotsa or me. And now my grandmother is gone."

"A shame that they couldn't have made amends before her death."

Heather shrugged. "Yes. I look forward to hearing whatever my mother has to say."

"And I can't wait to hear about it. I'm just sorry you have to wait until after my birth. Talk about pressure!"

"Not at all. There's no rush. Michael keeps asking me every morning if I'm leaving, and I have to remind him that there's not a chance I'm leaving until after your birth. You'd think he wanted me to be out of town." She smiled.

"How has Michael been doing lately?"

"He seems more agitated than usual. Perhaps that's why he's looking forward to having the house to himself for a few weeks. I don't really know."

Anna sighed. "I'm sorry. Sometimes marriage is difficult, isn't it?"

"Yes, I hope it's nothing more than irritation, and not that he's going to slip back into any old habits." Heather stood. "And now I must be going. *Wiiac*."

"*Wiiac*, Heather. Thank you for the visit."

After her friend had gone, Anna pulled out the journal Ben had given her the day he'd proposed.

She went back and read every entry, all the little and big adventures they'd had together since that special day. And there would be so many more, but now they would be a family of three.

With Comma curled up at her feet, she set the journal on her lap and closed her eyes, but then she heard Greta's voice. With a smile, she sat up.

Greta was walking around from the front of the house, and Anna could hear that a gentleman was with her, but not her grandfather.

The hair on Comma's back stood up, and he growled with a deep and angry sound in his throat.

"Don't be rude. They're visitors," Anna said, patting him behind the ears.

But when Greta appeared with Peter by her side, she froze as solid as ice.

"There you are!" Greta exclaimed. "I thought we might find you out here."

Peter smirked at her with great satisfaction, and Anna couldn't speak.

"Yes, your grandmother just served me the most delicious breakfast at her house. What a fine cook and hospitable woman." He bowed slightly to Greta.

"Well, when a gentleman stops by and says he's friends

with you and Ben, and that you were on the summit team together, I consider them family."

"He is not family," Anna said through clenched teeth. Her knees had gone weak, but she used her arms to lift herself up to standing.

Greta seemed confused and tried to help her out of the chair.

Peter laughed with twisted delight. "So, it's true. You're with child. And by the looks of it, you're ready to burst."

"Greta, this is Peter. He's the one who cut my rope and pushed Ben and I down the mountain."

Greta gasped and rushed to Anna's side.

Peter folded his arms over his chest. "Well, ya don't need to be afraid of me *now*."

Greta didn't take her gaze off of him, but she addressed Anna. "I'm so, so sorry, my dear. I didn't know—"

Anna put an arm around the woman's shoulder's protectively. "Of course, how could you have known."

"I only wanted to stop by and remind you where your place is. But now I can clearly see that you'll have good reason to stay home, what with a baby coming."

Anna shuddered. "Leave my property at once."

"Or what? Will you chase me out of here? I don't think you're in any condition for that. Being with child suits you. May you always be pregnant and within the confines of your own home." He lifted his hat ever so slightly, turning to Greta. "Ma'am, thank you kindly for the breakfast."

"You're going to get caught. You're smug and careless. And I've already been back to the mountain. You can't stop me from doing as I please." Anna crossed her arms over her chest and hoped that he couldn't see the beads of sweat forming on her brow.

"You have no proof of anything, no power over a man." He spit on the ground near her feet, then turned to amble away.

Once he had gone, Anna's breath came faster. Tears sprang to Greta's eyes, so Anna felt that she might have the strength to keep her head, but her hands were shaking.

After she had calmed Greta down and sent her back home, she locked the front door and sat waiting on the sofa until Ben returned from work.

Minutes turned to hours, until finally, she heard footsteps coming up their brick path. Heart racing, she peeked out of the curtains to make sure it was him before she undid the bolt lock on the door.

Once he was inside, she squeezed him tightly but couldn't come up with the words she wanted to say.

"What happened? You're shaking." Ben took his hat off and walked with her over to the living room, helping her into a chair.

After she'd told him everything, he scowled and reached for his bow from above the fireplace. "How long ago?"

"A couple hours now. Greta already went to the police on her way home," she replied, hoping her husband didn't plan to go out into the darkening evening to hunt down a man who knew how to surprise people.

"I'll just take a quick walk around our property—to make good and sure he's gone."

"But you won't go out searching for him, will you?"

"No, not tonight. Lock the door behind me?"

She gladly obliged, and once he was gone, she retrieved her bow from the closet and watched from the window.

# CHAPTER TWENTY-TWO
## NERVES

*Elizabeth | May 1892*

When Elizabeth returned to the hospital and offered to volunteer again, they invited her to join the hospital as an unpaid student nurse. That meant she would work a few hours each day to care for sick people in exchange for shadowing nurses and learning as she went.

As she was preparing to leave the house for her first shift, she checked on the tomato plants. The seeds they had planted were just sprouting, and it gave her more joy than she could have imagined. She watered them tenderly with North's dimpled smile in her mind.

The first week at the hospital went much more smoothly than she might have imagined. She spent much of her time replacing sheets and fetching water and soup for the terminally ill patients. She actually enjoyed herself around the elderly patients, as they proved quite kind if they were coherent at all. Many of them came from money—enough to get them months on end in a hospital, but not rich enough to be cared for by a dedicated nurse in their own homes.

Sometimes, she could sit for brief moments as patients had a meal. She could enjoy a quick cup of coffee, the mug warm against her palms, before hurrying off to perform more of the never-ending tasks in a hospital.

While she enjoyed being assigned to the floor she was on, she was hoping to see a few births. That was the area of medicine that interested her the most, and something she had ample experience with.

One afternoon, as she was cleaning the floor of a sleeping patient, the head nurse peered inside the room.

"One nurse couldn't make it in today. We need you downstairs."

Elizabeth smiled, her heart thumping. She propped the broom against the wall before quietly closing the curtain around the sleeping patient.

When she entered the floor, two nurses greeted her. One of them was the kind nurse from the time she had passed out— Meg. The other took her leave to join a different doctor on the other side of the floor.

"Welcome back to the hospital, Miss Grayson. I trust you're ready to learn today?" Meg asked.

Elizabeth felt a blush on her cheeks and chest. She was indeed, but even little opportunities like this always made her nervous. "Yes, thank you. I'm happy to help on this floor."

With a reassuring nod, Meg returned the smile and waved for her to follow and join a doctor who had just arrived for his shift—Dr. Roland. Elizabeth's nerves were tingling with anticipation for the rest of the afternoon. If she was lucky, she'd have two or three full hours before it was time to go home for the evening.

But she was nervous, of course.

The first patient they attended to had a broken arm, most likely. She watched while the doctor examined him, a young man in his twenties. He winced with each touch, his face white. Meg and the doctor used bandages to get the man's arm in a proper position to stay for a few days.

As they closed the curtain and walked over to a desk for the doctor to make notes, she wasn't sure if she should follow or give them privacy.

Meg whispered something to the doctor, and he turned around abruptly as if he'd forgotten she was there.

"Oh, right. Yes, please join us, miss. What's your name again?"

"Elizabeth Grayson, sir."

"Glad to have you . . . again, I think." The doctor glanced at Meg, as if to make sure that was what she had hoped for.

Meg grinned and motioned for Elizabeth to join them.

It was nice to be acknowledged, and she smiled graciously as she walked toward them. The doctor scribbled some notes on a paper and then waved them both forward to the line of patients behind curtains.

The next patient was an elderly Russian man groaning in pain. After a thorough examination, the doctor still did not know what the problem was. The man's broken English was difficult to understand.

The doctor turned his back on the patient and whispered for Meg to find a nurse who could speak Russian. After offering the patient another blanket and some water, they left his presence.

Elizabeth felt lucky so far not to see any blood, but she was bracing herself for the sight that would inevitably come on that floor of the hospital. She'd already decided what to do when it happened: focus on something else and pretend the sight didn't bother her.

The doctor's hair had streaks of gray, and she wondered if he was truly that old or if the stress of caring for patients had aged him. He didn't seem at all interested in conversation with the nurses any more than was required.

"I need some coffee," he mumbled as he scribbled down more notes.

"I'd be happy to go downstairs and bring some up. Would you like any, Meg?" Elizabeth asked.

The doctor's eyes lit up. "Actually, that would be marvelous. Thank you, miss."

Meg smiled and nodded as Elizabeth walked away. She could fetch a tray from the kitchen with coffee and biscuits. Perhaps she would end her shift being appreciated, which would bode well for being asked back to that floor.

She knew she couldn't stomach the energy of coffee at that late hour in the afternoon, but she needed water and nourishment for herself. She'd worked straight through lunchtime.

Even though nothing bad had happened yet, that familiar dread leapt on her back like a demon. She shook it off as she poured the coffees and took a long drink of water. Her stomach rumbled, so she devoured a biscuit as she arranged the tray. Sweating and heart racing, she went back up the stairs, happy that the shift was nearly over.

"What a delightful treat, thank you," Meg said as Elizabeth set the tray down on the doctor's desk. "We just may need you down here again next week as well."

"Yes, quite nice. Thank you kindly." The doctor drank half a cup of coffee with surprising speed.

Another nurse rushed up to the doctor. It was the one who had been unimpressed with her last time—Eleanor.

"The sweetest little boy at the end of the floor has split his lip right open. Can you see him right away? He's in a lot of pain and probably needs stitches."

"I'll be the judge of that," the doctor said, setting his mug down and buttoning his jacket.

Eleanor's lips tightened, and she glanced at Meg. Then they all followed him to the end of the floor.

The doctor flung the curtain open wide, and the boy stopped whimpering momentarily.

"How did this come to pass?" the doctor asked. "I hear you might need to see a doctor. How can I help?"

The red-haired boy was probably three years old and perched on the bed that seemed far too high for him. He made a pouty face and pointed to his swollen lip, which was quite a sight.

The mother wrung her hands. "He was jumping from one dining room chair to the other and hit his mouth on the corner of the table."

Elizabeth could already smell the blood. The doctor touched a finger to the boy's chin and lifted it. The boy opened his mouth and became a child-vampire with blood dripping down both sides of his mouth. Elizabeth's legs went weak and warm as the dread consumed her.

"Would be good for you to see this, Miss . . ."

"That's Miss Grayson, Doctor," Meg reminded him, motioning for Elizabeth to join him with an encouraging smile.

"Right, Miss Grayson. Have you ever seen a lip stitched up? You can assist me, if you like."

It was a privilege, Elizabeth knew. She had done well so far that afternoon, and he was rewarding her for it. He waved her over.

She nodded, fighting the nausea as she drew closer.

*Pretend. Just act as if everything is perfectly fine.*

Her heart was beating so fast, as if there were no time between beats, just a constant squeeze, her chest getting increasingly tighter.

It wasn't just that she didn't want to see or touch or smell the blood. There was something more—a deep-seated terror of it that made no logical sense. It angered her even as she remained a prisoner to her visceral response.

As she stood next to the doctor, she couldn't take a full breath, so she inhaled sharply and too fast. And just as she exhaled shakily, the little boy sneezed, splattering blood everywhere.

There came one moment between the sneeze and Meg laughing uncomfortably.

Elizabeth froze.

She had sprinkles of blood all over her arms and white shirt. Terror invaded her mind—everything inside of her revolted. It felt like her skin was tearing away from her body and the blood was burning holes into her, burrowing.

Conversation continued around her, but it didn't matter.

None of their words mattered.

She could hear loud gusts of wind but then realized it was her own rapid breath.

Eleanor had already fetched a water basin and a clean towel for the doctor. She handed a damp cloth to Elizabeth as she walked by her and patted her on the arm, not understanding the gravity of the situation.

After the doctor wiped himself clean, he looked over at Elizabeth, who still stood motionless, the cloth dangling from her limp hand.

Then he spoke, and she could tell he was talking to her, but she couldn't make out what he was saying. He turned away and stitched up the lip with Meg's help.

As she cleaned herself up numbly, she moved toward the hallway.

Soon, they were back at his desk, and Meg continued to wipe down Elizabeth's arms with the cloth. She dabbed at the spots on her white shirt, but it was useless. With a gentle hand, she used her own handkerchief to wipe the splatters off of Elizabeth's chin and her left cheek.

"You're terrified of blood. Why didn't you tell us this at the beginning?" the doctor asked.

Elizabeth didn't know how to respond, so she remained silent.

"Have you had fits of hysteria before?" Eleanor asked.

"No," she said quietly, shame filling her voice.

The doctor sighed, looking annoyed. "And it's fine. It really is. Of course, it's not surprising for a woman to be made faint by the sight of blood. This is why you nearly fainted last time, isn't it? It's all quite clear now."

"Well, it's certainly upsetting to have blood sneezed upon you," Meg said hopefully and with the greatest of intentions. "I certainly wouldn't have liked it."

The doctor frowned. "Young lady, it's fine. Nothing to be ashamed of. Your constitution is just weaker than that of others. We can still use your assistance with the older patients and other chores around the hospital. You mustn't quit on account of this. Of course, it's your choice. But you must have lied on your volunteer forms, because you certainly didn't like the sight of blood last time you were here. I remember that, by the way." Another severe look.

"This . . . is all just fairly new to me. That last incident and this. I'm so sorry."

His face softened. "Perhaps you can overcome it. Or perhaps your nerves will worsen and you'll need to make residence in an asylum for a time, to rest and get your strength of mind back."

Meg scoffed loudly, and the doctor gave her a stern look.

Elizabeth's insides twisted in despair. "I can overcome it."

It was providential that none of them had any inkling as to her obsessive behaviors in addition to the phobia. She knew the doctor wouldn't be so kind and forgiving if he knew the complete picture.

"Good. Well, I think you should put this behind you. But do return to your position upstairs. And stay there for the duration of your training this spring."

This shouldn't have surprised her, but she was still untangling from the shock of the incident, her muscles uncoiling like a snake. His words hit her like a runaway carriage, but she nodded somberly.

What would North think of all this? Perhaps it would be best not to tell him. He seemed so proud of her for being back at the hospital, and she couldn't bear to see him disappointed.

# CHAPTER TWENTY-THREE
## LATE

*Anna | May 1892 | The Tenth Month . . .*

As the first days of May dragged on, Anna resigned herself to the fact that her baby would simply never come. Heather had postponed her visit to the reservation for almost two full weeks, and every day that passed made Anna more anxious.

She hadn't seen anymore of Peter. It still made her ill that he was in her grandfather's house eating breakfast, chatting with Greta as if he was a regular gentleman and not some evil soul.

Anna stood in the kitchen, thinking about the strangeness of it all, when she saw Ben running up their road, papers in his hand.

He burst through the front door with the newspaper. "You'll never believe this."

"What is it?" she asked, unsure of what to expect.

"John and James wrote a piece about Peter. Well, about *you* and everything that happened."

"Who is James?"

"Elizabeth's brother. They both write for the *Seattle Post-Intelligencer.* Here, let me read part of it to you."

*In the sweeping aftermath of arson and attempted murder, Peter Beckwith has not only shown his true colors, but he returned to threaten Anna Chambers. Isn't it time for Seattle to be a place of peace and order, rather than a breeding ground for outlaws and miscreants? Women will have the vote in Washington as soon as we can get it approved—why then can men threaten an innocent woman for simply joining a mountaineering team? Women should be allowed to hike if they so choose. In fact, the new mountaineering club is made of both men and women, happily climbing together in harmony. This man needs to be found and his actions brought to justice.*

Anna was stunned into silence. She looked out their front window with the view of the mountain. Perhaps now that he'd been called out in this way, he might be more likely to be found.

Ben clenched his fists. "The police chief posted a new announcement, and they've been watching for him. And so have I. It's just a matter of time now."

Anna sat in a chair to get comfortable, putting her feet on a padded stool. "I need to find peace somehow, whether he's found or not. Plus, I have my bow in case he returns."

She smiled, thinking of the article. It was as if every friend and acquaintance had come together to support her. "I'm so grateful to them both for writing that."

Ben nodded. "I'll have to properly thank them."

She had been afraid to see him—even in her dreams—but now as she looked back on the past year she realized that his hate hadn't actually stopped her from doing anything. She had still summited the mountain after he tried to shove her down. She had even returned to base camp and helped found a mountaineering club that championed women. And now, this article petitioned the people of Seattle to support her and other women climbers.

It was more than she could have hoped for. She sighed and rubbed her swollen abdomen.

"And, I've decided something on a different matter."

"What's that, dear?" Ben asked, looking up with a question in his eyes.

"Heather just needs to leave. I can't bear to keep her here any longer when she could reconcile with her mother. And nearly being a mother myself, I know how important this trip is. I can't stand that it's my fault for keeping her!"

"It's not your fault. The baby will come when he's ready."

"All the same, I think I'll feel much better after she's gone."

The truth was, she was terrified to birth her baby without Heather, but it was also maddening to expect every single day to birth a baby yet have it not happen. And the waiting was made so much worse because it was delaying her friend.

"Let's contact Elizabeth and see if she can come over to assist with the birth. If it ever happens."

Ben laughed. "I'll get word to her right away. She'll be honored to be next in line to assist. But you'll have to tell Heather yourself. I won't be the one to tell her she should hurry and get out of town."

"I'm expecting her this morning. As soon as she arrives, I'll tell her. I've decided."

He nodded apprehensively. "Greta will be around too, and Emily."

"I know they mean well, but neither has attended a live birth."

Later, when Heather arrived, Anna told her.

"I understand why you feel that way, but it's truly not a rush," Heather said.

"I'm miserable, and the thing I want most is to have this baby and you be here, but I cannot keep you here any longer. Please, for me, leave today. Go speak with your mother. Please."

Heather sighed, crossing her arms and looking off into the distance.

"If that would make you the most at peace, I will leave."

She hugged her friend tightly, not wanting to let her go.

But Anna felt better after she had left, even though she despised the fact that she wouldn't have her there for the birth. Yet, it made the most sense. Hopefully, she would make it to the reservation that very evening.

When Emily showed up for her afternoon visit, she brought surprise guests: Adelaide and a few of her children.

"I hope you don't mind my bringing the little ones along," Adelaide said. She had two small girls holding both of her hands, and Emily held a bald toddler.

"Not at all," Anna said, smiling. "I'm so pleased with the distraction. Please introduce me to these beautiful young ladies."

The two girls giggled at being called ladies. One was only slightly bigger than the other, but they could have passed as twins. Their auburn hair was braided into two braids that hung around their shoulders.

"Nice to meet you, miss. I'm Kathleen. And this is my sister, Marie. She's shy."

"Well, it's a pleasure to meet you both," Anna said, leaning toward them as best she could with her swollen abdomen. "And how old are you, Kathleen?"

"I'm nearly six," Kathleen said, glancing up at her mother, who smiled encouragingly.

Emily plopped the toddler down on the grass. "And this hefty boy is Stuart."

Anna admired the good manners of the little girls, and a pang of longing filled her. She'd only dreamed of having a boy so far, but it seemed wonderful at that moment to have a daughter one day.

"And the two older children are at school," Adelaide said, spreading out her skirts and finding a place on the grass. "What a lovely space you have here, Anna. You must quite enjoy it. And your babe will probably love being out here as well in the fine weather."

It was something Anna hadn't even considered. She had imagined being in bed with the baby mostly, but Adelaide was right. The little one would probably also enjoy the fresh air and sunshine as long as she wrapped him up warmly.

"Why don't you girls help Stuart find some dirt to play in?" Adelaide said.

Emily reached for the hands of the girls. "I shall help!"

Adelaide's children weren't anything as Anna had imagined. After all the things her friend had said, she'd half-expected little devils. And Adelaide seemed to enjoy them too, and quite rightly.

Anna laughed. "Such delightful children you have. Did you have many siblings?"

"No, I was an only child. I always hoped to have lots of

little ones to surround me when I became a mother. And I've been fortunate indeed."

When they had spoken previously at the library association meeting, she had got the impression that Adelaide had a few too many children for her liking, and that they were quite the hassle. But this new vision of her sweet children playing in the sunshine, and her looking after them adoringly, was a much better scene.

"Can I ask you a question of a somewhat private nature, Adelaide?" Anna asked in a hushed tone.

"I don't see why not."

"You seem quite happy. Do your children make you so, or is it in spite of them?"

"Dare I say both?" Adelaide laughed. "Children are maddening and wonderful. They make me want to run for the sea and set sail, never to return, but I also miss them as soon as they let go of my hands. It's a mystery, I suppose, but I can't imagine life any other way. And I'm so grateful that my house is full of healthy little ones. But yes, I'm deeply happy."

Anna nodded, greatly reassured. She had no plans to have as many children as Adelaide, but it was such an encouragement to know that her friend was happy and living exactly the life she wanted.

"To be quite honest, the timing of this baby was disappointing," Anna said, shame turning her cheeks warm.

"I'm sure I was the same way—with most of them, actually. It never really seems like a good time to have a child. Until they arrive and you fall in love."

Anna grinned. If there was never a good time for being with child, she supposed now was as fine a time as any. It hadn't been what she'd hoped for, although she hadn't really planned in the first place. That she'd had to be so immobile might have happened no matter when she fell pregnant. Thank goodness she'd had the good fortune of summiting Mount Rainier beforehand.

So, she had hope. Just because the timing wasn't ideal didn't mean it couldn't work out perfectly well after all. And now she was quite grateful that her son or daughter would soon arrive.

THE NEXT MORNING, Anna awoke with a tightness in her belly. She reached for Ben's hand and put it over her stomach.

His eyes went wide. "My goodness. Does that mean he's coming?"

"I can only hope so. I've felt nothing like this so far. It's a lot of pressure."

"I'll alert the cavalry," he said, reaching for his pants.

She smiled. "I hope it isn't a false alarm, but I do feel different. Stop by and tell Greta first, please. She'll relay the message to Emily. And then fetch Elizabeth."

After Ben had left, she sat up slowly and swung her legs to the side of the bed. The pressure had come and gone and then come again, and she decided that while she had this break, she would dress and wash her face.

When she arrived at the top of the stairs, Heather's smiling face was poking in from outdoors.

"What are you doing here?" Anna asked, full of surprise. Then her eyes filled with tears.

"I would never let you have this baby without me," Heather said, entering and closing the door behind her. "But I thought maybe the pressure of trying to hurry and have the baby before I left was causing undue strain on you."

"So you let me believe you had left," Anna said, wiping the moisture from her eyes. "I couldn't be more pleased that you tricked me."

Heather smiled. "I was walking nearby and ran into Ben. Sounds like it's time."

Anna grinned and started down the stairs, slow and steady.

# CHAPTER TWENTY-FOUR
## A BURST OF BRAVERY

*Elizabeth*

The light came through Elizabeth's bedroom window at an early hour. The sheer curtains that covered them were delicate and didn't block out any light.

She shrugged out of her nightdress and dressed in her petticoats and skirts. She hadn't managed the courage to tell North what had happened recently at the hospital. Or the time before, for that matter. She wanted to, but the memories filled her with shame.

North seemed to adore her, but there was still so much he didn't know about her. She wondered what he would think if he knew the truth.

As she buttoned the tiny yellow buttons of her shirt, she thought of his sweet smile and encouragements and sighed.

North had invited her over to meet his grandmother that

morning, and it actually surprised her that the invitation hadn't come sooner.

When she arrived at his doorstep, she knocked on the door with butterflies in her stomach.

His grandmother poked her head around the side of the house, a wide-brimmed garden hat on her head.

"Hello there!" she said, waving Elizabeth over.

She was a tall woman with long gray hair streaked with dark brown in a loose French braid. Her eyes took Elizabeth in, and then she nodded with seeming approval.

She smiled warmly, then extended her hand. "I'm Clara. You must be Miss Grayson. It's a pleasure to meet you."

"Likewise," she replied, relieved. She wasn't sure what else to say. What had North already said about her?

North walked from around the corner, wiping sweat off his brow. "There you are. Grandmother has tea waiting for all of us inside."

"Your roses are lovely," Elizabeth said. The petals were a rainbow of different shades, but most of the buds were still tightly closed.

"Thank you, dear. North planted most of them for me," she replied, beaming. "Shall we go inside?"

"Yes, let's. Thank you again for inviting me over."

"I've been wanting to meet you for some time," Clara said, grinning. "But Northy has been keeping you all to himself, I suppose."

Elizabeth grinned at the term of endearment and glanced at him. He was blushing but offered his arm to both women.

Inside, there were lace curtains and a modest cookstove. It was a small house, and Elizabeth wondered how they had managed for the last fifteen years, especially before North started working for the railroad.

"Please, have a seat," Clara said, pulling out a wooden chair, then donning an apron. "I've got scones in the oven, and tea is ready."

The table had an enormous bouquet of roses in a wooden vase in the center. There were pink, yellow, and white roses all mixed, and the smell was divine.

"I hear you've been volunteering some time at the hospital. Good for you," Clara said, pulling a fragrant pan from the oven.

"Yes, I have," she replied nervously. She glanced at North, who nodded encouragingly.

"She's quite a skilled nurse already," he added.

Clara put a basket of scones on the table and poured tea for each of them.

"This china is lovely. Where did you get it?" Elizabeth asked, admiring the swirls of delicate painted flowers along the porcelain.

"My family brought it all the way from England," Clara said proudly. "Only one cup broke on the voyage over. They packed it so well with straw in a wooden crate."

"That's wonderful."

"Has North told you the history of our family?" she asked, glancing at her grandson as if for permission.

"I told her that my mother is probably back in England somewhere. And that Father died when I was a boy."

"But there's so much more to it than that!" she exclaimed.

North shrugged while Clara pulled her chair closer to Elizabeth.

"My grandfather was the head gardener of King George himself," she said with a pleased smile. "Everything from his magnificent rose gardens to planning and planting the very fruits and vegetables that the royal family ate. He was an expert gardener and passed down all his knowledge to me."

"And you've passed it down to North," Elizabeth said in awe.

"I have. Everything I know. And that's quite a bit, to put it modestly. I thought North would turn into a skilled gardener or a famous farmer in his own right as he got older, but he does still work with the ground whenever he can get away from work."

"I wouldn't be able to make a reasonable living as a farmer, Grandmother," North said, looking affectionately at her.

Clara looked at Elizabeth. "Once I started getting stiff hands and fingers, I had to stop working as a gardener myself. I worked at the Madison mansion. It just became too painful. That's when North dropped his schooling and got a job with the railroad."

"We take care of each other, don't we?" he replied.

"Yes, but I'm afraid I've robbed him of the full school experience."

"I certainly didn't mind," he said. "You know I hated school anyway."

"Suppose you did," she replied. "And now he's worked his way up to being a conductor, and I couldn't be prouder of my Northy."

Tears glistened in her eyes, and she wrung her hands before taking a shaking cup of tea to her mouth.

"That's a beautiful story, Clara. Thank you for sharing that with me," Elizabeth said, putting a hand on the older woman's shaking forearm.

"Don't you have a meeting at the church later this morning, Grandmother?"

"Oh yes, that's right. I should change and freshen up a bit. But I sure enjoyed meeting you, young lady." She grinned widely, apparently enjoying the blush spreading over her grandson's face. "Please come and visit again."

"Yes, ma'am. I will."

North breathed a sigh of relief as she closed her bedroom door, and Elizabeth smiled at him.

"She likes you," he said, one eyebrow lifted.

"I'm amazed at your history," she said, smiling. "And you never wanted to become a full-time gardener or farmer?"

"I probably could now, but I was too young when she first stopped working. I needed a job that made a reliable paycheck for us to live on. We don't have any other family in Seattle, or America, for that matter."

"I see. Shall we go for a stroll while she gets ready? And then perhaps we can walk her to her meeting?" Elizabeth asked.

North nodded and offered his arm. As they turned onto the pathway, Ben Chambers came running up to her, out of breath.

"Oh good, there you are. Anna sent me to get you. She believes the baby is coming."

"That's splendid news. You should get back to her quickly, and I'll run home and get some things and meet you there."

He nodded with an anxious look and then hurried away.

"Your presence is required elsewhere," North said with obvious disappointment. "Allow me to walk you back to your house."

She fell silent, not knowing how to voice what she wanted. She was delighted for Anna, but she knew there would be blood, and the idea made her want to stand frozen and never move again.

At that moment, she wished that she'd already explained to North what had happened the last few times she'd seen blood, but she was too embarrassed.

"For some reason," she said hesitantly, "blood terrifies me lately."

"Well, blood can be scary."

"Right, but when I see it or smell it or, even worse, have to *touch* it, my brain absolutely freezes. I feel like I'm dying, and my brain thinks of all these awful things that could happen and probably already have happened because of the blood."

"Whoa, that's serious," he said, sounding more interested. "Will there be much blood at a birth?"

"Not necessarily. Some, yes. Possibly a lot. It just depends, really."

"My goodness," he said in a low voice. "Well, you *want* to be there, right? You've mentioned in the past that you love being present and assisting with births."

"I absolutely do. I love it. I just haven't been present for a birth since this new fear has come."

"Oh, blood hasn't always bothered you, then?"

Elizabeth shook her head. "I think it was the day of the earthquake. Or around that time, rather. But ever since I bandaged someone up that day, every time I see blood, my nerves get the better of me." And then almost too quiet to hear, she added, "And my nerves are bad enough as it is."

"Then you just need to summon your courage, I think."

She swallowed hard. As if it were that easy. As if just wanting to be there, wanting to be a nurse or birthing assistant, could make all the ridiculous fear disappear. She said nothing in return.

"I know it must be hard," he said finally. "But blood is a normal part of life and certainly a normal part of working in medicine. Maybe it would help if you think about it logically, apart from how your body's reacting."

"It helps to think of it logically, but I still get frozen to the spot, and my body and brain just . . . do not want to cooperate."

He blew out a breath.

Elizabeth let go of his arm to wring her hands together. Did he think her insane?

"Can you really be a nurse if you can't handle the sight of blood?" he asked with some trepidation.

She mulled that over. It was still her dream to follow in the footsteps of Florence Nightingale. She wanted to assist in births and the time after, where blood would always make an appearance, even if peripherally. Still, she didn't know what to say, but she looked at him with a serious expression and nodded.

"Think of it like this. Do you want to be a nurse *more* than you're scared of blood?" he asked.

"I think so," she replied.

"Then, Liz. You can do this. Go to Anna, and make the choice that you're going to assist, no matter what. You *are* going to be a nurse, even if you have to feel uncomfortable and downright undone a couple times today and in the days after."

She didn't quite believe him yet, that it could work, but a smile came over her face. For one, he wasn't judging her, but also, he was encouraging her to fight through her fears. Something about his confidence in her was empowering, energizing, and she felt a burst of bravery.

"Okay. I'll go at once," she said with a spring in her step, the energy pinging around inside her.

# CHAPTER TWENTY-FIVE
## IT ALL COMES DOWN TO THIS

*Anna*

"Your grandfather has fallen ill," Ben said when he arrived home breathless. "Greta is taking care of him, and the doctor is going to go by their house this afternoon."

"What's wrong with him?" Anna asked in alarm.

"He has a fever and a nasty cough."

She hadn't expected Greta to be much help for the birth specifically, but now that she couldn't come, it made her sad. But more importantly, she was worried about her grandfather.

"Is he going to be alright?"

Ben sighed. "He's a strong, healthy man, isn't he? I should expect he'll be just fine. I can go check on him again this evening and let you know how he is. Also, Emily is there to help."

Anna nodded. That would have to be enough, for now anyway.

"But I found Miss Grayson, and she promised to be here shortly."

"Thank goodness." Anna expected that between Heather and Elizabeth, she was in worthy and skilled hands.

Another wave of tightness surrounded her belly, and she sat back in her chair.

"Should you go lie in bed now?" Ben asked, biting the inside of his cheek.

Heather came into the dining room with a tray of teacups and a steaming teakettle. "There will be plenty of time for lying in bed later on. For now, she can do whatever makes her comfortable."

"Can I go outside?"

"Of course. Would you like to take your tea in your garden?" Heather asked.

Anna nodded. She could think of nothing more peaceful than to begin her laboring journey in her haven. Necessity had forced her to spend time there instead of enjoying more active outdoor activities, but now she was fond of the place.

Ben sighed, crossing his arms, but he nodded and reached a hand down to help her from her chair.

The spring air swirled around her as she stood at her front door. The scent of blooming lilacs and grass grown tall greeted her nose. As she sat in her chair, the mountain stood crisp and proud high above, and yet so far away. Snow covered almost every visible inch of the great peak, giving her a sense of cool beauty.

Just before she took a drink of her tea, her belly tightened again. "They still don't come very often."

"That's perfectly fine," Heather replied, taking the seat opposite her.

The sound of footsteps preceded Elizabeth as she came around the house into the backyard, her feet moving with purpose.

"Here you are," she said, looking around at the garden. "And this is lovely."

"Thank you. And many thanks for coming to assist. I can't say there's much to do yet, but your company is dearly welcome."

Elizabeth looked up at the mountain. "She makes a beautiful sight today. I like how you have your chair facing something you love so much, especially for this new experience."

Anna grinned. Yes, Heather and Elizabeth would make a great team for her.

They passed the afternoon in the sunshine among the birdsong and gentle breezes. Elizabeth prepared a light meal of cheese and tomatoes for Anna so that she could keep her strength up in the time ahead.

"How many babies have you helped bring into the world now, Heather?" she asked her friend.

"I suppose seven, including June's sweet boy," Heather replied with a far-off smile. Then she turned to Elizabeth. "I hear you have much experience with births as well. Along with some practice with procedures in the hospital. That's excellent."

Elizabeth blushed. "Heather, have you ever considered delivering babies as a profession? To be honest, I've been thinking more and more of it, but I'm not sure how one starts out doing that officially."

"Officially?" Heather shrugged. "I help friends and family

with their births, but I'd never considered doing it for anyone else. It would certainly be enjoyable."

"I think so too," Elizabeth replied.

Ben came in and out of the house, seeming more concerned with each passing hour.

He appeared outside again to give her a kiss on the cheek, and Anna could see the worry in his eyes.

She whispered in his ear, "You're supposed to be the calm one, remember?"

"Oh dear, you're right. My apologies. I had just imagined this going differently, and it's thrown me off."

"Perhaps you could check on Grandfather?"

Having a task to do would calm his nerves. Thankfully, the peace of her haven was working its magic. And even though the birth was coming soon, it still seemed in the distance because she was outdoors.

"Yes, I can do that. Right away." He spun around and marched toward the Gallagher house.

But nearly ten minutes later, he returned with Emily by his side. "Look who I ran into on the way."

Emily smiled until her gaze landed on Elizabeth, then her face fell. Anna cringed at how apparent the reaction was, which was actually a welcome distraction from her own situation.

"Hello, Elizabeth. I wasn't expecting you here, but it's good to see you."

"You as well," she replied, looking down at her tea.

"Thank you." Emily stalled, swallowing and then looking up to Anna. "Oscar is still feverish, and the doctor had just arrived when I left."

"Whatever is wrong with him? Can you tell?" Anna asked, concern growing in her spirit.

Emily shook her head. "He woke up in a terrible sweat this morning and has been sleeping most of the day. We've been keeping his temperature down, though, and we hope the doctor will have answers. But I have other news as well, Anna."

She couldn't imagine what else could be of much import to her at that moment, but she lifted her eyebrows in question.

"It's Peter—a man who runs a saloon on Madison Street turned him in to the police. My father brought word of it to me this morning. Said to tell you at once, but I didn't want to leave Greta's side until the doctor had arrived."

A man had turned Peter in.

*A man.*

He must have read the article in the paper.

How dramatically things had changed since bricks were being thrown into the bookstore. People seemed to be on her side now. Or at least on the side of justice. It made her heart swell.

"This is excellent news about Peter," she said, taking Emily's hand. "Thank you for telling me. It gives me strength."

Emily nodded. "My father said that he'll be made to pay for the damage done at the bookstore. And, I'll come back as soon as I can with word about your grandfather. Try not to worry."

And then she turned away.

"Well, there goes my task that would have made me useful," Ben said with a half-smile. "But what good news about Peter being turned in!"

The hardest wave of pressure yet hit Anna, and she moaned as she closed her eyes. Enduring the moments of pain reminded her of being on the mountain, fingers and toes nearly numb from the cold, lungs aching, muscles crying out for rest.

Yes, she knew then as she knew now. It was but a temporary struggle that would lead to something great—something bigger than herself. The reward would far outweigh any pain it took to get there.

"I think I'm ready to lie down now," she said, looking at Ben. "Would you be so kind as to help me into bed?"

He sighed gratefully. "I'd be delighted, my dear. I thought you'd never ask."

She chuckled.

As they walked up the stairs, there was a lightness in her chest despite the weight of her current earthly body. Peter would have to account for his actions, but more important than that was the fact that her own town was starting to come together on the side of women.

But then she thought of her grandfather, and her stomach turned. So much had been going on, and it was easy to focus on everything but the fact that he lay feverish, in and out of restless sleep.

They still didn't know what ailed him. He had seemed to age more and more lately, but she had thought little of it. Now, it weighed on her heavily.

She knew that if her grandfather had been more coherent, he would have insisted that they withhold news of his own illness until after she had delivered the baby. And so it worried her even more, knowing what a terrible state he must be in.

# CHAPTER TWENTY-SIX
## THE MOMENTS AFTER

*Elizabeth*

Awaking from a quick nap on the couch, Elizabeth blinked rapidly. The sun was rising and the house was quiet. Anna had labored through the night, and Heather had insisted that Elizabeth get some rest before the morning hours.

She went outdoors to gather the dry blankets from the line, then returned with a basketful. Her mind wandered to North and how calm his voice had been.

She couldn't smell blood at the moment, and so she took a deep breath, eyes closed, pulling the bravery out of her bones before she walked up the stairs.

*I will stay in the room for this birth.*

When she entered Anna's bedroom, all of her senses were at attention as the room was abuzz with movement in all directions, like a well-oiled machine. Ben held Anna's hand.

Heather moved to the other side of the bed. Elizabeth unloaded the fresh blankets on the edge of the mattress.

She paused a moment at the foot of the bed, breathing deeply, a rhythm that matched her own heartbeat, five beats in, five beats out.

Inhale.

Exhale.

"Her water broke," Heather announced calmly.

That meant blood.

*"Liz. You can do this. Go to Anna, and make the choice that you're going to assist, no matter what."*

His words calmed the tightness in her chest. In just a few brief hours, possibly less, the baby would be here, and everything would be cleaned up perfectly. All would be well.

She returned her focus to Heather, who nodded encouragingly to Anna, reminding her to breathe. Elizabeth also released a shaky breath, squaring her shoulders.

The yellow blankets, the smell of soap, the wind rustling the curtains by the window—she let those concrete things ground her. She was attending another birth—she would be a nurse—she was going to be braver than her fear.

"I see the head. You're doing great, Anna," Heather said with apparent delight.

Elizabeth placed the blankets where the baby would come and stepped back to let Heather catch the baby. She could see a small sliver of dark hair matted with blood emerge into the world.

Her knees weakened, but she widened her stance. She tried her best to keep watching, to give words of encouragement.

She shifted her focus—away from herself and onto the birthing mother, and on the child working to come into this world alive. That was all that mattered.

"It's a girl!" Ben exclaimed, his voice cracking.

Heather covered the baby with a blanket and put her on Anna's chest. She had already wiped away most evidence of the birth from the bed, which Elizabeth couldn't possibly be more grateful for.

But she was soaring from the fact that she had actually done it—nowhere near the feat that Anna had accomplished, but still. She was light-headed, and a chair in the corner enticed her. She moved toward it, blinking repeatedly.

North would be impressed. She was quite proud of herself.

But before she could feel too pleased with herself, she realized that there had been little blood. At a hospital, the potential for constant brush-ins with blood would be near constant.

"Elizabeth, can you fetch Anna a glass of water?" Heather asked, breaking her thoughts.

"Of course, right away."

She returned quickly with a large glass of water and some biscuits. Now it was time to make a more substantial meal for the new mother.

As she set the water and biscuits down by Anna's bed table, she peered down at the infant.

"Congratulations to both of you," she said. "She's beautiful. Have you chosen a name yet?"

"We're going to call her Grace." Anna grinned, glancing from her baby's face to Ben's and then back to Elizabeth. "Thank you so much for all your help today."

"My pleasure. Truly. Now, if you could have any meal in all the world, what would it be? I will make your wish come true."

Anna laughed. "I'm quite hungry but also exhausted."

"Well, the dinner of your dreams takes time, so you've

plenty of time to rest while I prepare it. Think about it for a moment, and I'll be back to take your order."

It was a tradition Elizabeth held fast to, and she quite enjoyed doing it.

"I'm so grateful I was here for the birth," Heather said.

"You're the dearest friend," Anna said, eyes twinkling with moisture. "Now you should get going and start your journey to the reservation before it gets too late in the afternoon." She turned to Elizabeth. "Are you free to stop by occasionally over the next couple of days? Just in case I have questions?"

"Absolutely," she replied with a smile. "I'd be delighted to. And yes, Heather you should get on your way. I'll get everything squared away here and prepare a meal for the new family."

Heather hugged Anna and admired the baby for a moment longer. She made sure the baby was suckling properly and then took her leave.

"For a meal," Ben whispered to Elizabeth, "if you really don't mind, I think Anna would enjoy pancakes."

"Pancakes?"

"Yes, she loves them. With whipped cream and strawberries, if you can find any this early in the season."

Elizabeth grinned. "I think we might have had an early shipment from northern California come in by train. I'll be back soon."

With that, she bid her farewell and put her light shawl over her shoulders.

As the bell above the door jingled her arrival to Grayson's Grocer, her father greeted her with a wide grin.

"Good to see you, darling," he said with gusto. "How did the birth go?"

"As perfect as can be," she replied.

"Glad to hear it. You were made for that kind of thing."

She beamed. "Thank you, Father. Do you have any fresh strawberries?"

He tilted his head. "You're in luck. Just got a small shipment. Let me grab some from the back. Did your mother ask for them?"

"No, I'm making a meal for the Chambers family."

She looked around the store while he went to the storage area in the back. The place looked different to her after the earthquake—with a different feel to the air. She vividly remembered the way the ground had shaken and the counters rolled. Being as she stayed most of the night for the birth, she wasn't that steady on her feet as it was, so she leaned against the counter to steady herself.

What about that day had caused her to be afraid of blood so badly?

So many things had happened at once, but it was only the little boy's cut that had spilled blood that she could recall anyway.

There had been panic and confusion, but she'd kept her head and tended to everyone nearby that needed help.

Perhaps her mind had been in the perfect state to attract a little demon of fear. And now she couldn't shake it. There seemed to be a correlation to her new fear of blood and the condition of her nerves at the time of the earthquake, which was shortly after Levi's letter, and the rejection of Dr. Glazier.

This felt like a revelation. Knowing her own mind was half the work of staying sane. Her spirit had been heavy with worry, rejection, and the earth actually shaking—and it had brought to life a new fear that she'd never had before.

Her father returned with a small basket of strawberries and a grin. "I hope the new mother enjoys them."

"Thank you so much. I have no doubt she will." She kissed her father's cheek and then pushed the wood door open, the sun greeting her face as she walked outside.

She glanced to the wood-planked sidewalk, over where the boy had dripped his blood. There wasn't a spot to be seen now. She wished that knowing where the fear had come from would make it disappear, but it didn't. It was a relief to see that the blood had disappeared.

Back at the Chambers' house, all was quiet. Both Anna and the baby were sleeping, but Ben greeted her at the front door.

With a yawn, he motioned for her to come back inside. "We're indebted to you, Miss Grayson. I don't mind making some food, though, if you'd like to get home. I know it was a long night for everyone."

"Nonsense. You go sleep with your family, and I'll have food ready in a while. You may have a disjointed evening again tonight, but I'll sleep soundly."

Ben laughed and thanked her again before slowly walking up the stairs.

Elizabeth got right to work in the kitchen, whipping cream and slicing strawberries. She'd wait an hour to start the pancakes, since they wouldn't take long, and she knew Ben and Anna needed their rest.

She looked around the kitchen to see if there was anything else to be done that might make their lives easier in the coming days. First, she got to work on dough for some bread and started chicken soup to have on the stove that could be served whenever they liked.

In what seemed like no time at all, she heard the sweet infant whimpering, which turned into a full-on wail. Then she heard Anna calling her name.

"Is everything all right?" she asked at the door.

"Do come in," Anna called.

When Elizabeth pushed the door open, she could see the baby bobbing at Anna's breast, not finding what she was looking for and getting angrier by the second.

"Heather just put her right to it, and she seemed to know what to do," Anna said, eyes still sleepy. "Can you help?"

"Of course." Elizabeth came to her side. All the while, Ben slept on. Perhaps he'd sleep through the night just fine after all.

"Here, you'll just need to guide her a little. She knows what she wants to do, but you have to get her right on the spot first."

"Thank you," Anna said with a sigh. "I'm so glad you could stay a bit."

Elizabeth nodded once the baby latched properly. "Glad to help. I'll have some pancakes with whipped cream and strawberries ready shortly."

"That sounds incredible!" Anna said with a dreamy look on her face. She glanced down at her baby, and the smile only grew bigger. "She's perfect, isn't she?"

With a nod, Elizabeth said, "Absolutely."

*They all are.*

# CHAPTER TWENTY-SEVEN
## THE PROMISE

*Anna*

Anna greeted the sunlight with relief. She had already been up several times to feed her baby, but it felt more human to wake during daylight hours.

"Do you suppose Greta and Emily will visit today? Any word on my grandfather?"

Ben hesitated as he came in the front door. "He's weak, but he's nearly recovered. The doctor said it was diphtheria."

"How long did the doctor say until we can visit?"

He exhaled and then frowned. "A few more days at least, maybe longer. Greta was sick for a couple days, but she's better now. And Oscar is over the worst of it. But it's weakened him considerably."

The tears came once again to her eyes. It had been an emotional week already, with the birth and the days after.

The timing was all wrong too. Greta and her grandfather should have been over visiting the day that Grace had been born.

But the doctor had insisted they quarantine until the illness was behind them.

And even as her grandfather's fever had faded and the coughing diminished, Greta relayed that his complexion was paler than ever, and he hardly had the energy to sit up in bed.

The thought put a sinking rock in Anna's stomach that threatened to take her soul with it to the depths.

For as long as she could remember, he had been the solid family pillar she had depended on. He tied her to memories of Ireland and her parents. His presence alone was as peaceful as the heights of the mountain.

She wiped a tear from her cheek and then kissed Grace's soft, warm head. It was a comfort to hold the babe in her arms.

"Also, there's more news about Peter. His trial will be in a few weeks. It seems most likely that he'll owe a large sum for setting the bookstore on fire, and many city residents are petitioning that he be sent away from Seattle."

Anna breathed a sigh of relief. It was all good news.

"It's more than he deserves," Ben said, his upper jaw rippling as he ground his teeth. "I should give the man a visit in jail and—"

"Actually, I'd like to visit him," Anna said. "Not today, but before he's sent away."

What a gift she'd been given. It was more than she could have hoped for. His own foolish choices had led him to where he was now. And not only that, but by his extreme actions, he'd made it seem far more reasonable to support a mountaineering woman than a violent, hateful man.

A knock sounded at the door, and Ben answered it to find Elizabeth standing in her hat and gloves.

"Good morning, Ben. Are you off to work?"

"Yes, I need to get going." He kissed Anna's cheek and then put a finger to Grace's cheek, smoothing it to her tiny pink lips. "I love you both. See you this evening."

Elizabeth started water boiling and kneaded the dough she had left sitting to rise overnight.

Anna watched her work with gratefulness she could hardly express. It would have been Greta or Emily doing these things, spending this time with her after the baby was born, but she was lucky to have Elizabeth willing and able to be with her.

"You know I'm forever indebted to you for all your help," she said.

"Nonsense. I quite enjoy taking care of mothers and babies. I won't hear of any *debts* regarding the matter." She smiled, looking up from the dough.

Anna realized how much the girl had seemed to grow over the past few months. And especially since she'd first met her— the quiet, timid girl on Levi's arm.

She remembered back to Elizabeth's letter, when she had shared the same opinion regarding morning sickness not, in fact, being caused by the mother not wanting her baby. She had first felt a gladness for the girl then, but now a genuine friendship was blossoming.

"I haven't asked you about this, but I was wondering your thoughts on something," she said without looking away from her sleeping baby.

"What is it?"

"Do you suppose I did something to cause the bleeding I had at the beginning? I mean, could it all have started because of my choice to go up to base camp so early on?"

Elizabeth smiled and wiped her hands on a towel. "Even with the most docile women, bedrest is sometimes needed. I don't believe the cause of the bleeding was anything you did or didn't do. It's just the way of it sometimes."

"But the doctor did recommend that I don't walk around so much, and that it would slow or stop the bleeding. And that worked. I guess I just wonder if—if it was possible I could have lost her, pushing it too hard on that trip."

Shame filled her, and she could barely look up at her friend.

Elizabeth came to sit beside her, admiring the baby in her arms. "I think we lose babies for all kinds of reasons, mostly having nothing to do with what we imagine. But you were lucky that your body sent you warning signs and you heeded them. And all that matters now is that you have a beautiful, healthy baby girl in your arms."

She nodded as Elizabeth patted her arm and then rose to finish the bread.

"Have you thought about what you'll say to the man in jail?"

Anna scoffed. She was both dreading and looking forward to confronting Peter at the police station before they sent him on.

"There are so many things I'd like to say. So many things I've told him in my dreams. I guess I'm not quite sure what will actually come out of my mouth when I see him again."

She'd had so many nightmares reliving the terrifying fall. It was almost hard to remember the actual scene. The terror of the knife pushed up against her coat. The feeling of flying as she was weightless and falling down the mountain. The jerk as the rope caught around Ben's waist and sent him flying after her, to what might have been both of their deaths.

Two weeks later, the time came. Emily's father, Mr. Watson, had arranged for Anna and Ben to visit Peter. It felt odd to be separated from her baby for the first time, and she still had some soreness, but most of the bleeding had stopped, and she couldn't wait any longer to say her piece to him.

But when they arrived at the police station where Peter was being held, the building front was charred and black—smoke rising from the roof.

Mr. Watson stood to the side with other police officers who were helping the firefighters.

They went directly to the group, and Mr. Watson took them aside.

"We believe he must have set fire to the jail himself last night, or early this morning. He was the only one inside."

"Did he escape?" Anna asked, her throat catching. There was so much she had planned to say to him.

"No, he's dead," Mr. Watson said, crossing his arms over his chest. "We didn't even get to bring him to trial. And I'm afraid there's no way to get that money that would have gone toward your family bookstore."

Ben put his arm around Anna's shoulders.

The news came as quite a shock.

She had wished him dead. She had believed that a simple fine and a banishment from the city was too lenient.

Why had he cared so much about women climbing mountains?

She imagined how he might have responded if she'd asked him this in person. Perhaps he would have spit on the ground near her feet and looked back up at her in silence.

He knew that she was coming to see him today—Mr. Watson had informed him.

Did he prefer death to being confronted personally? Or had he only set fire to the jail as a means of escape, but failed?

She shuddered.

As they began to walk away from the scorched shell of the police station, Anna felt a relief deep in her soul.

A WEEK LATER, the doctor finally cleared Oscar of his illness and Greta and Emily from any potential contagion. Ben and Anna came to visit and to introduce their baby to everyone.

"Oh my!" Greta said with delight as Anna put the baby in her arms. "She's lovelier than I've been imagining."

Emily and Levi rushed toward them both. One by one, everyone expressed their congratulations and spent their time admiring the newest addition to the extended Gallagher family.

"Where's Grandfather?" Anna asked, looking around the living room. He was nowhere to be seen.

"He's upstairs in our bedroom. Are you ready to see him?" Greta replied. "He can't wait to meet his great-granddaughter."

Anna nodded, preparing her heart, but knowing she'd never be ready to see her grandfather in such poor shape.

Ben, Levi, and Emily stayed in the living room while Anna and Greta climbed the stairs. Greta knocked softly on the door. "Darling? Anna has brought her precious babe."

Inside, the room was dim. It smelled of cinnamon, vanilla, and the deep forest.

Her grandfather was propped on pillows and thus sitting up. "Bring that sweet lassie into my arms. I've been waiting ever so impatiently to meet her."

Anna grinned as she placed her in his arms. Close up, her grandfather's eyes were bloodshot, and his face was as white as she'd ever seen it.

"Now that's a bonny girl," he said, winking down at the baby. "I think you'll be just like your mother, and her mother before that."

"Well, we certainly hope so," Greta said, beaming.

"Why don't I hand her back to you, eh? My arms are weaker than they used to be."

Anna nodded and scooped Grace into her arms. "I hear you're making gains toward recovery."

He chuckled. "I'm as strong as an ox. I'm sure that's plain to see."

"You will always look strong to me," she said, tears forming in her eyes.

She handed her baby to Greta, who tiptoed out the door humming a lullaby.

"Anyway, I think you'll be good as new in no time, Grandfather."

Oscar looked down at his hands with a straight face. "I wish that were the case, lassie. But nothing brings me greater joy than knowing both you and Levi have made families of your own. You'll take care of Greta, won't you?"

She reached for his rough, warm hands and put them to her cheek. "There's still time, Grandfather. Let's not talk of that yet."

He stared at her for a long while, then nodded. "You had a tough time being with child. It wasn't like that for your mother, so I had no way to know or warn you."

"Everything worked out alright. Now it's over, and I'd do it all again to have Grace with me anyhow."

"You sure made the best of it. I'm proud of how you found

a place for yourself despite being stripped of all your favorite things. You found joy being a lady in the Library Association, and simply resting in your own garden."

Anna smiled softly. She had finally made peace with the timing of her pregnancy and all she'd had to give up to bring her daughter safely into the world. "Thank you."

She kissed his cheek and wanted to talk more, but she could see how tired he'd become from the conversation. "I'll bring Grace up to say goodbye before we leave."

He closed his eyes and smiled. "Please do."

Downstairs, Greta had served a platter of pickles, cheese, and sourdough bread, warm and toasty from the oven. Emily was in a rocking chair snuggling the baby, and Anna knew it wouldn't be long before her friend had a child of her own, making her an aunt.

When it was time to feed the baby, Emily returned Grace to her mother, and Anna took her to the porch, to her favorite spot in the house—with a view of the mountain.

Tears filled her eyes for what seemed like the hundredth time over the past few weeks, and she simply let them fall as she rocked and nursed. When she lifted Grace to sit her upright against her chest, her tiny baby fingers wrapped around the cameo at Anna's neck. She locked eyes with the baby, and it seemed as if Grace knew more than she let on.

"I promise I'll take you up there one day," Anna said, wrapping her hand around the baby's fist that still clung to the cameo. She looked up at Mount Rainier, knowing that such joy still lay ahead.

# CHAPTER TWENTY-EIGHT
## THE CARRIAGE RIDE

*Elizabeth | June 1892*

North was coming that evening to escort her to a fancy dinner at a restaurant, and so Elizabeth was scouring her closet for the dress that would make her feel her best.

The weather had been fickle, so she wasn't sure if she should wear a summer dress or prepare for rain. Gray clouds were rolling in from the ocean, and that always meant a solid shower was coming. But perhaps it wouldn't come until the late evening. Maybe the June heat would leave her damp and uncomfortable if she overdressed.

Still uncertain, she opened her bedroom window and put her hand out to get a sense of the wind and humidity. A large raindrop landed directly on her palm, which settled it.

Helping Anna with her sweet baby had been satisfying work. She hadn't been able to spend as much time at the hospital, but she knew there would always be sick people there needing help when she was ready to return.

By the time the carriage arrived, there was an all-out downpour. North came to the door with an umbrella, but the wind was blowing from every direction. Elizabeth couldn't help but laugh at how damp she was when she settled into her seat.

"Oh dear, let me fix your hair," North said, leaning toward her.

"I'm not sure there's any help for it," she replied, feeling for the chignon under her hat.

He brushed away the wet strands of hair that seemed to be plastered around her face. The sensation brought a tingle down Elizabeth's spine.

"I can't wait to take you to this place," he said, settling back in his seat. "I've always wanted to go but never had anyone special enough to take there."

"You flatter me," she replied, trying not to let the power of his words show visibly on her countenance.

The door of the carriage rattled, and she reached over to make sure it was closed all the way. It seemed to be shut, so she withdrew her hand. Then again, she had the need to feel it completely shut. Without thinking, she touched it again.

When she realized North was watching curiously, she sensed a pink flush starting on her chest and then creeping up to her face. She looked out the window and was silent.

"What just happened there?" he asked, perplexed.

"Did you hear that a new play is going to be starting next week at the theater? I'd love to go."

He was silent.

She looked up at him meekly. "What did it look like to you?"

"I don't quite know, but I saw how embarrassed you got, so I know something happened."

"Would it be possible to just pretend it was nothing? And never speak of it again?" she asked.

"Liz, I want to know you. All of you. Everything about you. Why do you want to hide anything from me?"

She exhaled loudly, exasperated, and dug her heels in. "It's just that it's not important. It's nothing I wish to share with you, at least."

His shoulders sagged and his eyes looked pained.

She regretted upsetting him, but perhaps the courtship had gone as far as it needed to go. It would break her heart to say goodbye to him, but it couldn't be helped.

When she looked up to see his face again, the carriage swerved, and then they began to float. At first, she wasn't sure if it was her nerves or if it was real, but then she realized she was suspended in air, and North was too, until the carriage crashed onto its side.

She landed on top of him in a terrible collision of limbs and seat cushions. Her head landed squarely on North's stomach. But he hadn't fared so well.

When the motion had stopped, everything was dark, and the only sound was the thick rain pouring down on the sideways carriage.

Footsteps came running, splashing toward them, and the door was opened directly above her, letting dim evening light and rain inside.

"North, are you alright?" she asked, trying to find his face in the weak light.

There was no answer, and she frantically reached for his torso and up to his face. She got as close as she could and realized his eyes were shut. But worst of all, blood now covered her hands.

It was pouring out of a gash on his forehead.

Her arms went numb as the panic took over. But this time she didn't know what scared her more: the blood or the very real possibility that North was dead.

A man's voice came from above—the driver. "Are you alright down there?"

Elizabeth was still trying to gather what had happened. The carriage must have hit a rock, and with all the water streaming through the streets—it was hard to know exactly.

Another man, presumably a passerby, reached his hand down. "Let me help you up, miss. You'll have to jump up a little, but we can get you."

"No," she shouted. "You both must right the carriage as gently as possible. There's a badly injured man with me, and I won't be able to get him up through the door."

The two men looked at each other and then disappeared.

Panic consumed her, but she didn't wipe the blood away. The carriage swayed as they attempted to lift it back upright, but it didn't matter because the universe was spinning anyway.

She remembered how she had focused on Anna and her baby when the fear of blood had threatened to freeze her. That was the key—keeping her mind on what was actually happening, right now, rather than retreating into the abyss of her mind.

She cradled North's head in her lap, attempting to keep his neck steady through the jostling. Blood poured out of the gash on his head with every pulse, which might have horrified her even more, except that he still had a pulse.

With every surge of blood, she rejoiced until the carriage was upright. She quickly reached for the bottom of her petticoats and tore off a long piece. She made quick work of winding it around his head to cover the wound and attempted to stop the bleeding, or at least slow it until it could be properly stitched.

That was when she realized how badly her own arm hurt. A dull, throbbing pain came from her shoulder, as well as a wretched sharp pain in her elbow. And blood still covered her hands, but that was the least of her worries.

Rather than struggling to wipe her hands or turn away from North's bloody face, she focused on him, watching for any twitch or facial expression that might show he was regaining consciousness.

None came.

❧

AT THE HOSPITAL, Elizabeth woke in a bed of her own. Everything was clean and crisp around her. Even her fingernails had been scrubbed of North's blood. She sat up at once, looking in every direction, but curtains surrounded her. As she lifted her torso up to lean on her elbows, the sharp pain in her arm made itself known.

A bandage went from her upper arm and nearly down to her wrist. The pain was great, but her panic to see North overcame everything else.

She heard footsteps walking by and called out. "Excuse me! Nurse?"

Meg rushed into the room and ran to her bedside. "I'm so glad you're alright. Only a broken arm and nothing more, I believe. How are you feeling?"

"Where's North? The man who was in the carriage with me?"

"He's being stitched up now, but I have to warn you, he's in terrible shape. Hasn't woken up yet, and his leg is broken as well. After they stitch up his head, they'll need to set that leg. I suppose it's a mercy he isn't conscious."

Elizabeth began to cry. The shaking of her shoulders made her arm scream with pain, but she couldn't make herself stop.

# CHAPTER TWENTY-NINE
## EXPOSURE

*Elizabeth*

Elizabeth refused any medication for her pain. She wanted to be awake as soon as there was any news about North's well-being.

She awoke early the next morning to her family visiting her.

Her mother rushed to her side. "You poor thing! We're so grateful you're alright. Any word about Mr. Bailey?"

Elizabeth shrugged helplessly, tears forming again in her eyes.

"I'll go see if I can find out anything," James said, pulling the curtain to the side.

Meg walked in and shook her head. "We don't know anything yet. But we're taking good care of him. He's resting now."

Elizabeth's father kissed her head and then stroked her hair back. "My sweet girl. What would we do without you?"

Meg brought a sling to her and began fitting it on her arm. "You'll want to wear this as often as possible. It will take the pressure off your arm and shoulder. Are you well enough to go home with your family this morning?"

"No," she stuttered. "I mean, I'm fine, but I have to stay and wait until North wakes up."

"You must come home, dear," her mother said.

"I'll stay here with North," James said. "I'll send word the minute he wakes. Would that be alright with you?"

Elizabeth nodded shakily. It would be better to rest at home, but she knew it would feel like peeling away part of her own flesh to leave North at the hospital, not knowing when or if he would wake.

"Can I have a moment to see him before I go?" she asked Meg.

"Of course. I'll help you dress while your parents fetch a carriage. Then I'll take your brother and you to him."

Later, when they made their way down the corridor to the area where critical patients were, the smell of blood permeated the air.

When Meg pulled the curtain back and motioned for them to go in, Elizabeth caught sight of North's pale face. A large bandage wound around his head, and his leg was bandaged as well.

She reached for his hand and squeezed it. The touch proved reassuring, but without his movement to touch her in return, it felt ominous.

"I'll watch over him," James promised, sitting down on a wooden stool in the corner.

Just as she turned to go, a doctor came into the room.

"Meg, please change the bandage on Mr. Bailey's head, and reposition his leg."

"Will he be alright, Doctor?" Elizabeth asked, her voice cracking.

She vaguely recognized the doctor, but she'd never worked directly with him at the hospital. He looked down at her with pity.

"We're doing all we can, miss, I assure you." Then he sighed. "The gash on his forehead extended into his hair line, but we got it all stitched up, and the bleeding has stopped. It was good that someone bound the wound when they did. He wouldn't have even made it to the hospital otherwise."

Elizabeth inhaled sharply, and Meg glanced at her.

The doctor continued. "His broken leg will heal in good time, but I'm more worried about the head injury. I don't know what's going on in there, and it's not a good sign that he's still unconscious."

Elizabeth nodded with as much bravery as she could muster. "But there's a chance he could make a complete recovery, isn't that right?"

The doctor nodded slowly, lifting his eyebrows. "Yes, yes, I've seen it go both ways. The young man certainly has a chance."

When he left the room, Meg smiled. "You bandaged him up, didn't you, Elizabeth? And that's why your hands were blood-soaked."

She nodded quietly.

"I scrubbed them as clean as I could while you slept. Didn't want you upset upon seeing them when you woke. But I suppose you wouldn't have minded it, being your beloved's blood and all."

"That's disgusting," James said, making a face.

Elizabeth managed a smile. It was true, though, that when it had mattered most, she hadn't let the fear consume her. Taking care of someone in need—the most important someone—had been imperative.

But now she didn't know if he would even live.

She bent down and kissed North's cheek before spinning around to leave the room.

Later, her mother helped her into a carriage to take her home.

When they arrived, she noticed the rhododendrons were blooming in their front yard. Pink and magenta colored the landscape, which made her think of North's grandmother.

Elizabeth chided herself for not thinking of it sooner.

"Mother, I don't think she even knows, since North hasn't been awake to tell them."

"You rest, dear. I'll visit Clara and make sure she knows to go to the hospital."

Elizabeth washed her face as best she could with only one arm and then lay on her bed, looking up at the pink canopy.

The dark scene played again and again in her mind. The feeling of suspension, the tumbling, the hard landing. Then nothing but stillness and the sound of the rain.

She turned onto her good arm and wept. They should have never gone out in that downpour. Perhaps if they'd been sitting on the same side of the carriage, North wouldn't have fallen so far. The scenarios played out in her mind of how the accident might have been avoided altogether.

And to think she had been about to tell him that their courtship should be over. Over what? Him knowing about her secret?

But now, after experiencing the possibility of losing him forever, she knew that she'd never prefer that over the risk of telling him the truth. It was a risk she was willing to take, but now it might be too late.

And just at that moment, her brother burst into the door. "He's awake! And he's asking for you. I have a carriage waiting."

She sat up at once, wiping the tears from her face, then followed her brother down the stairs and into the carriage.

When they reached his hospital room and she threw the curtain aside, she found Clara at North's bedside.

When she locked eyes with North, she knew that she'd found the one her soul needed.

"You saved him!" Clara exclaimed and ran to Elizabeth, throwing her arms around her. "The nurse told me everything, and I can never thank you enough."

North reached his hand toward her, and she took it.

"I heard it was pretty bloody. But you're a nurse, so you handled it." He winked and tried to sit, then groaned.

His grandmother put a gentle hand on his shoulder. "You need your rest, my dear. But I'll leave you two alone so you can reconnect."

She kissed North on the cheek and then hugged Elizabeth again before shutting the curtain behind her.

Tears came to Elizabeth's eyes as she leaned in close to North, sitting on his small bed.

"I thought I lost you," she managed to say.

"I felt like I was losing you right before the crash."

She shook her head and wiped her tears away. "Everything has changed now. I can't possibly imagine my life without you anymore."

"I'm glad to hear it. But you don't have to tell me your secrets if you aren't comfortable. I understand that."

"How about I change this bloody bandage for you first?"

"Yes, ma'am," he replied, laying his head back against the bed.

As she unwrapped the bandages, she looked away from the blood, but its power seemed to have less of a hold on her as before.

"Are you sure it doesn't bother you?" he asked kindly.

"I can manage. And I wouldn't want anyone else to do it besides me anyhow. Well, I suppose Meg can if I'm not around." She smiled down at him.

"So, do you think you'll try your hand at being a nurse again?"

"I think I prefer delivering babies and helping to take care of mothers after the birth," she said, grinning as she thought of Anna's beautiful little one and how happy she'd made the Chambers family with her help. "There's blood to be dealt with, but the precious life that comes in the end is worth it. I think I just need a good enough reason to endure the blood."

"And perhaps with time and more exposure, you'll discover it doesn't bother you as much," he suggested, touching her arm softly as the last bandage fell.

"I wouldn't complain about that one bit," she said, reaching for fresh bandages. "And what about you, Mr. Train Conductor? I suppose you won't be able to do your job thoroughly for a few months at least. The doctor said your leg is broken in two places."

"Yes, I suppose I'll take a long time off. Maybe Grandmother and I can sell our seeds and produce. It's not too late to plant a surplus."

"That sounds wonderful," she said. "Perhaps I'll speak with Heather about going into the midwife business together."

When she finished the fresh bandages around his head, she kissed his forehead. "I have fits of panic sometimes. As far as I can tell in my research, I might have something called the doubting disease. The fear of blood was just new this year. It came about just before I met you, while I had a lot weighing on my mind."

"A doubting disease?"

She smiled, finally feeling comfortable enough to speak with someone about it. "I know it seems strange, but even after I have snuffed candles out, or put water over the fire, I doubt that I have. Sometimes it helps to touch it, or maybe that makes it worse. I haven't figured it all out yet."

"It's fascinating. Thank you for sharing it with me." He took her hand and she became still. "Is there anything I can do to make things easier for you?"

"Not really," she replied with a grin. "But now that I've said it all aloud . . . it just feels good to tell you about it—for someone else to know my secrets, I guess."

*What would he think of all this?*

In the silence, she laughed nervously. "I'm pretty strange indeed, when it's all laid out. A life with me would be full of challenges."

"I can handle challenges," he said. "Let me be the one by your side—you can trust me to keep your secrets. And when you panic, I'll wrap my arms around you. I don't know how to solve the doubting, but I'll be there for you whenever you need to talk about it."

He put both of his hands on her cheeks and then looked down at her lips. When they kissed, the world was silent, peaceful, and still.

# EPILOGUE
## RIPPLES AND REFLECTIONS

*Anna | August 1906 (14 years later)*

Anna watched her daughter step into the stagecoach, then followed her inside. The girl's long dark hair was so much like her own, but she had her father's soft brown eyes.

The train behind them whistled as it pulled out of the station at Ashford. The stage coach jostled while Ben and their blue-eyed son, Oscar, entered.

"A train ride all the way to Ashford and a horse-drawn buggy to Longmire Springs," he said with wonder, rustling the light brown hair of his son next to him. "How spoiled we are."

"Taking a coach is our tradition," the boy said with a scowl, looking up at his mother. "When will we arrive at the mountain?"

She smiled at his eager expression. "We'll take a tent at the new National Park Inn near Longmire. And then we can hike from there up to the Camp of the Clouds tomorrow morning."

"The tradition is to go to the mountain every summer, not walk for three days on flat ground, just to get to the base of the mountain," Grace said, folding her arms over her chest. "It's high time we used more modern methods of travel. Plus, the best part is camping on the mountain anyway, and this just gets us there faster."

Ben smiled at Anna and nodded. "Your sister is right, Oscar. She's been making the trek for some time now."

At just fourteen years old, Grace had joined her parents to camp under the stars in the alpine meadows nearly ten times. But Oscar was only nine.

"I'm thrilled to check out the new inn," Grace said, looking out the window at the horizon. "There's a French chef, and the tents have wood floors and electric lights."

"I thought we'd all enjoy the tent better than a room at the inn," Ben said.

"Oh yes, definitely," Grace said, nodding emphatically. "And I can't wait to tell my friends all about it."

"I don't understand why we can't climb past the Camp of the Clouds this year," Oscar said with a disappointed whine.

Anna and Ben exchanged glances.

"Well, perhaps this year we can go as far as the snow line . . . and just a little farther," Ben said, winking at his son.

"Really?" Oscar asked, his eyes shining.

"Susan Longmire was able to summit the mountain when she was twelve, and here I am at fourteen and being slowed down by my own little brother," Grace said, sighing with distaste.

"Well, no one's stopping you! Maybe you should start the climb up there all by yourself tonight—"

"That's enough," Anna said, smiling as she looked out the window. "It won't be long now until we can all go as a family as high as we'd like to."

The idea of taking both her children, along with Ben, to the summit of Mount Rainier gave her unspeakable joy. It was such a cherished tradition to take them up to the base camp every year to hike and camp under the stars.

"And in a few years, the road will be ready for touring cars to take us from Ashford to Longmire," Grace said.

"Imagine that, Anna," Ben said, leaning forward with his elbows on his knees.

She shook her head in disbelief. She could still remember walking beside mules on the dusty path with tall grasses all around them, with the farms in the distance few and far between. The twentieth century was already full of possibility and ingenuity.

The thirteen miles to Longmire Springs went by relatively quickly. Next to the newly erected National Park Inn, the old hotel looked positively run down. It had just opened in July of that year and boasted thirty-six rooms, not including the fashionable tents next door that could house another seventy-five people. The tents had walls, doors, and electric lights all across from the bubbling springs that made the area so popular.

Early the next morning, they set out toward base camp, each with their own small packs. Deep blue sky was wide above them, and Anna admired each serene landscape they came to. The Nisqually Glacier was a sight to behold, and it always impressed young Oscar.

Without pack animals, the crossing of the Nisqually River was considerably easier. Now, with tents and supplies to rent at the Camp of the Clouds, it wasn't necessary to hike with it all.

Above the roaring river, a fallen tree had been turned into a genuine log bridge. The width around the log made Anna believe it had been hundreds of years old before it finally succumbed to the proximity to the river and made a full tilt across the expanse, its ball of roots rising into the sky in an impressive, towering heap.

Atop the log were proper boards and suspended railings, so she felt comfortable letting her children cross. She stood in wonder in the middle of the bridge, remembering the times when she had walked beside mules, trying her hardest not to be swept away or hit by a rushing boulder or tree stump.

"I can't wait to get to the ice caves," Grace said, her eyes shining with anticipation.

Anna had never imagined that anything in all the world could top the feeling of discovering the beauties of the mountain. But watching her children admire the same beauty brought a kind of satisfaction she couldn't describe. Grace was in awe of the glaciers, their deep blues and cavernous insides. Oscar delighted in the alpine views and dreamed of flying like an eagle above the land.

When they came upon the ice caves of the Nisqually Glacier, she could see ridges of ice in what looked like a long hill coming down the mountain. As if the dormant volcano had at one time spewed ice and rocks and it had frozen in its great descent. Boulders of varying size were strewn about the entrance to the cave, but Grace couldn't be stopped as she scurried over them and into the cavernous depths.

Inside, it was as if they were in the underbelly of a long-forgotten castle, with arches leading into dark paths. The inside walls of the cave were shiny with ice, and pockets of lumps of ice gave texture to the arched ceiling of glacial expanse above them.

"It's magical," Grace said, her head flung back, admiring the blue lights above her illuminating the ice cave around her.

"It is," Anna replied, putting an arm around her daughter. "I hope you can share this place with someone you love one day."

Even with making stops at Narada Falls and Carter Falls to wonder at the lovely beauty, they made good time as they always did.

The alpine meadow opened before them as they drew closer to the base camp, and flowers of every color painted the soft grasses with color. Pink daisies entertained white butterflies while lazy honeybees visited the purple lupines. A small gray bird made a dive in front of Anna, then landed in the underbrush, making gentle hops as she landed.

All the glorious colors stood starkly against the white of the mountain looming above. And when they came upon the lake of reflections in Paradise park, Anna's breath caught. The beauty of mountain lakes was no surprise, but somehow, every time she came to this one and saw the peak of Mount Rainier reflected so beautifully, so truthfully, in the still water, her soul was captivated with joy.

Ben slipped an arm around her lower back, resting his hand on her hip as Grace and Oscar scrambled to the bank of the water to look at their own reflections and make faces to laugh at. Anna put her own arm around his back too, and she leaned into the side of his chest.

"I think it becomes more beautiful each time," Ben said, pulling her close.

"I couldn't agree more."

He pulled out four pieces of wrapped chocolates and handed them out to his family.

Anna grinned, unwrapping her delicious morsel. "Oh, it has an elephant on it! That's new."

"A new candy mold for an old-world chocolatier. But it tastes the same as always. Scrumptious."

With her mouth full of chocolate, Anna laughed. As she watched their children walk around the lake, she remembered back to that summer when she was carrying Grace inside her.

She had sat on the rocky bank of the lake, looking up at the mountain, at the deep green evergreens surrounding her, and at the reflection of the mountain itself. At that time, doubts had consumed her. She'd worried about her ability to be a good mother and the idea of taking care of a young soul.

She wished she could go back and tell her younger self not to worry—that everything would work out beautifully. And perhaps her own love of the mountain would cause ripples in the generations to come. She imagined her daughter bringing her own husband and, one day, children to see the beautiful reflections of paradise, and it filled her with hope for the future.

❦

## THE END

# ABOUT THE AUTHOR

*Author portrait by Melissa Nolen*

Jamie McGillen lives in the shadow of Mount Rainier, and no matter how many times she moves away, it draws her home. Everything about large evergreen trees delights her, except how poky they are, and the sap.

Her poems and essays have been published in numerous literary journals, and she teaches English Composition at Highline College.

She also loves to chat with readers, so say hello on Instagram, send her an email, or leave a review and you'll make her day! (Every time you leave a review for this book, a baby book angel gets its wings. Don't deprive them, for heaven's sake.) You can connect and find out more about her at www.jamiemcgillen.com.

instagram.com/jamiemcgillen

facebook.com/jamiemcgillen

# BOOK CLUB QUESTIONS

1.  In what ways are misconceptions about motherhood and pregnancy still harming women today?
2.  Which event in the book was most similar to something you've personally experienced?
3.  Do you know anyone who is dyslexic? If so, have they grown and overcome that hurdle?
4.  Do you have any phobias? Can you remember when it started?
5.  Anna volunteered for the Seattle Library association. Have you ever volunteered at your local library?
6.  Which character was most like someone you already know? How did that affect your perception of the character?
7.  Have you ever felt stuck between protecting your family and living a fulfilling life?
8.  What surprised you the most about this book?

9. Which character did you relate to the most?
10. Did you agree with all of the decisions Anna made? Would you have done things differently?
11. Which of the leading men in this book would you most likely fall for?
12. What do you think is in store for Elizabeth in her future?
13. Were you satisfied or disappointed with how the story ended?

# ACKNOWLEDGMENTS

I owe a large debt of gratitude to my fearless beta readers: Jillian, Peggy, Melton, and Gabby. This story would not have been the same without your collective input. Thank you.

Zee, Christy, and Amanda: Thank you for your editing, proofreading, and moral support.

Richelle - Thank you for the beautiful foreword.

Thank you to my wonderful launch team: Abi, Alejandra, Ally, Amanda x2, Anya, Ashlee, Ashley x2, Brenda, Brittany, Brittney, Cara x2, Char, Cindy, Colette, Crystal, Danielle, Elsa, Emily, Esmeralda, Eve, Gabby, Hannah, Holly, Jenny, Jessa, Joanna, Katie x2, Kimberlee, Lauren x2, Leigh, Leighellen, Lindsay, Lisa, Mary Ellen, Megan x2, Michelle, Missy, Nicole, Rachel, Rebecca, Riley, Samantha, Sandra, Sarah x2, Shereen, Sierra, Stef, Stephanie, Sue, Tristan.

Claire - Thanks for being my writing bestie4life.

Shawnasy - Putting the launch boxes together wouldn't have been nearly as much fun without you. Thanks for all your help over the last few weeks.

Megan - Thank you for being the president of the #jamiemcgillenfanclub. I named the nice nurse after you!

Mollie - Thanks for walking in the sunshine with me.

Honeymooner - Thanks for your enthusiasm, and your firm belief that I am awesome. You're my forever favorite.

Scott - You just keep getting funnier and taller. Thanks for being the best son ever.

Rachel - I love you. I like you. I love being your mom.

And a final thanks to my brilliant grandma, Barbara Pavitt, who passed away while I was writing this book. I miss you.